HER HUSBAND'S MISTAKE

DANIEL HURST

www.danielhurstbooks.com

Her Husband's Mistake

Download My Free Book

If you would like to receive a FREE copy of my psychological thriller 'Just One Second', then you can find the link to the book at my website www.danielhurstbooks.com

Her Husband's Mistake

PROLOGUE

I know the woman behind me still has her gun pointed at my back, so that's why I prefer to keep looking ahead whilst praying for a miracle. As I do, I see the murky waters of a large river flowing in front of me, and it's a river that has witnessed a miracle once before, though I fear there shall be no such repeat of any miracle here today.

A skilled pilot was once able to land a large aircraft full of passengers on this river I stand in front of, after dozens of birds had been sucked into the engines shortly after take-off, saving hundreds of lives and making himself a hero in the process. But I am no hero, or heroine, to use the correct term for my gender, and I'm not trying to save anywhere near as many lives as Captain Sully did.

I am only trying to save three.

Those lives are mine and my two children's.

But as of this moment, it looks like I am going to fail on all counts.

As I draw in a deep breath, well aware that it will be one of my last, my eyes move across the Hudson and fall upon the spectacular sight of the city that this river cuts through.

Staring at the solid masses of steel that make up the numerous skyscrapers in the New York City skyline, I think about all the people inside them and the view they must have from being so high up. Soon these buildings will be shimmering with electricity as the sun sets and their lights turn on, though it's a sunset I will not get to experience myself.

I'll be gone by then, as I fear my children will too, and that confirms my worst fear.

I have failed as a mother.

I have let my kids down.

And now I am never going to see either of them again.

As I close my eyes and shut out the unique view, the iconic city is replaced by pure darkness, and I prepare for that darkness to be permanent. But despite being terrified, I can't say I am shocked. That's because a part of me always knew that one day, I would have to pay for my part in what happened in New York before.

A mistake was made here, and while it was a long time ago now, I always knew it would come back to haunt me.

So it has proven.

I knew I shouldn't have come back here. I should have stayed in England where my conscience was a little clearer. But I came back, along with my family, and because of that, we have all had to suffer.

So why did I come back here if I knew it was a risk?

The answer to that is a simple one.

I was simply trying to be a good mother, and a mother will do anything for her children.

As the woman behind me prepares to shoot, I'm just about to learn that the hard way.

Her Husband's Mistake

ONE DAY BEFORE NEW YORK

1

LORNA

'You're going to the Big Apple! I'm so jealous!'

I have no choice but to move my phone away from my ear to lower the volume of the excited squeals coming from my friend, Beth. It's either that or hang up and end the call, but that would be very harsh because my friend is simply excited for me and the holiday I am about to take.

As she put it so exuberantly, I am going to the Big Apple, the nickname of NYC, the city that never sleeps, which is apt because I've always been a terrible sleeper myself. It's been that way my whole life, from being an excitable child who hated going to bed to being a young mother raising two noisy kids and all the way to the present day, being a woman in her mid-forties with all the lessons of my life very much on my mind even though I wish some of them could be forgotten.

'Are you all packed?' Beth asks me once I've put the phone back to my ear and braved her loud voice again.

'Not yet. That's one of the many things on my To-Do list.'

'What? Aren't you flying tomorrow?'

'Yep.'

'And you're not packed? What have you been doing?'

Beth's question is an innocent one but also the kind only a person without children would ask. She and her partner, David, decided not to even try and go down the route of having offspring, meaning that Beth's life now is pretty much the same as it was when she was in her twenties. She goes where she pleases and does whatever she wants; she sleeps in until whatever time she likes on a weekend, and she doesn't really have to think about anybody other than herself, though I suppose, occasionally, she considers her partner. Even then, the biggest question they have to answer is which takeaway should they order from tonight.

She wants to know why I haven't packed yet.

Here goes…

'Where do I start?' I say with a sigh. 'I had to drive to the passport office in Liverpool to collect Maddy's new passport because her old one had almost expired and she hadn't noticed until the last minute. I've been driving Alex back and forth into Manchester all week because he's started taking acting classes there. And I was up late last night trying to find an affordable travel insurance policy for us all because I remembered that I hadn't sorted our cover yet, and the last thing I need is one of us breaking a leg in New York, leaving us having to pay extortionate medical bills. It was past midnight before that was done, and then I just collapsed into bed.'

I'm breathless at describing just a few of the many activities that have kept me occupied this week, and that's all on top of holding down a full-time job, trying to keep the house tidy and making room for five minutes in my hectic schedule to greet my busy husband, Jack, and ask him how his day has been.

'Oh, I see,' Beth replies, now a little more understanding of why I've not put a single thing in my suitcase yet.

'Yeah, it's been a bit of a mad week so far,' I confess before I check the time and realise I have to leave the house in ten minutes to go and pick up Alex again.

'Okay, I just wanted to call to wish you a nice holiday, and I can't wait to hear all about it when you get back!' Beth cries, her exuberance returning. 'Have fun and send me a few photos! Oh, and make sure you come back, please. I almost lost you to that city once before, and I'll be damned if it takes you away from me again!'

'Thank you. I'll be coming back, don't worry about that. Speak to you soon,' I mutter before the call ends, and I go in search of my car keys.

As I do, I think about a couple of the words Beth used then and how they really don't apply to me in this case.

Holiday. Fun.

While it might seem that way to my friend, I know this is not a holiday, at least not for me, and it certainly won't be fun. That's because I really don't want to go to New York and neither does my husband. We're only making this trip for our children, and that's another thing Beth doesn't understand about being a parent.

It requires sacrifice.

And I am certainly making a sacrifice with this trip.

The reason the four of us are jetting off to America tomorrow is because there are a couple of big birthdays this year in my family and those due to celebrate them have made their request for what they would like as a present. Maddy is due to turn twenty-one in a couple of months, while Alex will be eighteen only three weeks after that, making this a momentous year in the Thompson family. As such, I always knew it was going to be an expensive time, though I didn't quite appreciate just how expensive it would be until my children told Jack and me what they wanted as their presents for reaching such milestones in age.

They wanted to go to New York.

Or rather, they wanted to go *back* to New York.

As I finally locate my car keys and head for the front door, I feel my stomach churn as I think about the city this family used to call home. It's a shame that such a magnificent place is forever tainted in my mind, after what happened there just before Jack and I made the decision to move back to England, because there was a time when we adored NYC and felt fortunate to call it our home.

It was 2002 when Jack accepted the job offer he received from a bank in New York. He worked for the same bank in England but this was Head Office calling him, and this new role overseas meant a big promotion and pay rise. Perhaps more importantly for his future prospects, it meant he would have a desk in a prime spot in close proximity to the CEO and managers of the bank who had the power to make him just like them one day. Career-wise, and being as ambitious as he'd always been, it made sense for him to take the offer, and Jack was quickly sold on the idea of swapping the UK for America. But I was a little more hesitant for a couple of reasons. One, it was only six months since the 9/11 attacks had brought New York to its knees, so I was understandably a little apprehensive about moving to a place that had been the scene of such an atrocity. But two, and this was the much bigger reason, I had been pregnant with Maddy at the time, so I wasn't sure how I felt about becoming a new mother in a foreign land.

Jack and I spent many nights staying up late debating whether to stay exactly where we were, in the sense of both geographically and financially, or make the leap and go to New York, new baby in tow and all. In the end, he persuaded me to chase the American dream with him, and I said we would go, though I had one stipulation. He would have to delay his start date with the New York office a little because I wanted to give birth to our daughter in England. Jack agreed; Maddy arrived three months later, and while she was practically still a newborn, the three of us boarded a plane and headed for JFK Airport.

What can I say about our start to life in America? It was certainly different. New York is an amazing place to visit, but to live there? That takes a little getting used to. Everything in that city is so much bigger, brasher and bolder than anything in an English city, and if people think the tube in London is crowded, just try getting a subway at rush hour in NYC. But as Jack had told me it would be, it was also an adventure, and the more time that passed, the more I fell in love with my new life on the East Coast.

Jack's employers paid for us to stay in a hotel in Manhattan while we looked for somewhere permanent to live, and that meant the first few months of motherhood felt like something out of a movie. I would push Maddy's pram around Central Park at lunchtime. I would grab a coffee near Times Square and enjoy my drink before giving my daughter her next feed. And I would stand at the hotel room window and try to soothe my crying child while looking out at the top of the Empire State Building only a few blocks away.

It was crazy, but it was so much fun, and as Jack's career thrived in his new office, I felt like I was thriving in motherhood too. That's why, just two years after Maddy, I decided I wanted to give her a sibling and a year after that, our son arrived. But again, I had the stipulation that I wanted to give birth in England, so all of us flew back as late as it was safe to do so, and I had our boy in more familiar surroundings, with family and friends nearby. We called him Alex, a name inspired by the star player for the New York Yankees baseball team at the time - Alex Rodriguez - a team Jack had grown fond of after attending several games with his work colleagues. Then it wasn't long until we were back in New York as a family of four, and things carried on as well as they had done, the years quickly rolling by and life going so well that Jack and I often contemplated if we would ever move back to the UK permanently.

But then we reached a pivotal year in more ways than one.

2008.

Most people, particularly Americans, would associate that year with the financial crisis that saw the US housing market collapse, several banks and institutions fail, and the beginning of a global recession that led to everybody suffering to some degree, no matter where they lived or what they did for work. Being at the epicentre of it all at the time was certainly a unique experience, and I'll never forget the sight of so many people in smart suits literally crying on the subway one day while I was with Alex and Maddy. It was also brutal to see Jack come home from work every night and tell me some shocking stories about clients at his bank who had lost everything, as well as listen to him voicing fears about what might happen to the bank itself in the long run.

But despite all that craziness, and it was a very worrying time, that is not the reason 2008 will always be a terrible year to reflect on for me. Something else happened that year, something that hit much closer to home and was much worse than overpaid, risk-taking investment managers losing everybody's money. It was something so bad that it caused Jack and me to leave New York and return home with our family as quickly as we could, while at the same time vowing never to go back.

He made a mistake, and it was a terrible one.

But I made one too.

And I still haven't forgiven myself for making it since.

As I leave the house and get in my car, ready to face the traffic to get into Manchester city centre and pick up Alex from his acting class, I still feel that awful aching in the pit of my stomach. It's the one that I've had ever since my children told me what they really, really wanted for their big birthdays this year - now that they were adults, they wanted to go back and see the city they had spent the first few years of their lives in.

I said no at first. I said the same word again several more times. But my children were adamant. A trip to New York was all they wanted, and if Jack and I wanted to mark their big birthdays in the best way, we knew what we had to do.

We had to take them back to that city.

But while going there is unbelievably exciting for our children, going back is extremely daunting for their parents. I fear going back to New York may be the second mistake of our lives, and the first one was big enough.

The first one almost ruined us.

My kids still don't know it.

But my husband and I certainly do.

2

JACK

Last night's football scores are currently being read out by the reporter on the radio, but I'm paying little attention to that as I drive along the motorway. I'm also paying little attention to the speedometer until I see a police car on the bridge up ahead and suddenly realise I'm going ten miles per hour over the limit and need to slow down.

I do just that before moving out of the fast lane and into the slower middle lane, and as I pass underneath the bridge, I am confident I have avoided the attention of the police officer this time.

I seem to have a habit of lucky escapes when it comes to the police.

Not wishing to dwell on that fortunate but grim fact, I turn the radio up and try to lose myself in what the reporter is saying. But just like a moment ago when I was inadvertently speeding, I am finding it incredibly hard to concentrate on anything other than my impending trip to America.

As the football scores are concluded and the reporter moves on to talk about tennis, my mind flits to a sport I never thought I would be interested in until I spent some time living in New York. Baseball is huge there and it became a big part of my life, so much so that I named my son after my favourite Yankees player at the time. But I no longer follow the baseball scores, just like

I no longer think about all the guys I used to go to the Yankees games with. They were guys who were colleagues and good friends, but they all disappeared into the distant past once they realised that I wasn't particularly eager to reply to their Facebook messages asking me how my life was after I'd moved back to the UK.

As I see the sign for Lancaster University, I signal to come off the motorway before moving onto a quieter road, slowing my speed considerably as I go while making another attempt to push all thoughts of New York out of my brain. But while I have mostly managed it well over the last fifteen years, it is almost impossible to do it when I am due to fly to that city tomorrow morning.

My hands grip the steering wheel tightly as I take several deep breaths and tell myself that everything is going to be fine. But at the same time, a little voice in my head also laments the fact that my children have forced me into this difficult situation. I love my kids and would do anything for them, and being aware that 2023 meant two big birthdays for them, I was always prepared to spend big to give them exactly what they asked for.
But then they went and asked for the one thing I did not want to give them.

I'd rather my children had asked me for a car or even a deposit for a house - expensive things but far more palatable than me setting foot in NYC again. I'd happily have paid for a trip to Australia if they wanted that, even though it would have cost a fortune and meant two days on a plane flying there and back. It's not that my children are spoilt and can have anything that they want, it's just that I've done well in my banking career and have the savings to make their dreams come true, so why wouldn't I help do that for them?

Unfortunately, what they are dreaming of is the one thing I wish I could not give them.

They want a return to New York to see the places where they grew up.

As I drive through the tiny village of Galgate and see the big university looming on the hill ahead, it's the skyscrapers of NYC that are looming large in my mind. Not just that, but I'm also visualising the flash of the yellow taxis on the crowded streets, the hum of the subway underfoot, and the bright lights of Times Square as numerous loud and colourful videos play on all the big screens.

Seeing all that in my tired mind is enough to make me want to pull this car over by the roadside and be sick out of my window.

That's before I even think of a police officer with an NYPD badge on his uniform.

I swallow hard as I push the policeman from my mind and turn into the entrance for the university, entering the place where my daughter has been a student for almost three years now. Maddy is in her third and final year of her Economics degree and once she graduates this summer, hopefully with honours, there will no longer be a need for me to make the journey up here every few months or so.

The first time I came here, all four of us were in the car, and it was quite the eventful journey. My usual chatty

18

daughter was quiet during the drive, excited but pensive at moving out of home for the first time. Her brother was much louder, chattering away about how he was going to take over Maddy's bedroom now she was gone and teasing his sister about enjoying her being away. Then there was my wife sitting beside me in the front passenger seat. Lorna didn't make it obvious to any of us, but I noticed she was wiping away a few tears as we moved along the motorway, and those tears were being shed because she was going to miss Maddy the most. There is no doubt that was an emotional day for all of us, and we hoped that Maddy would settle in quickly in her new surroundings, as well as all trying our best not to feel too sad about getting to see her less than we were used to.

Maddy did settle well, and it turned out that I didn't have to worry at all about not getting to see much of her because I've been back here several times since, whether it has been to bring her home for the holidays or to drop off an emergency supply of food because she has spent all her money in the student bar again. I've had no problem making the forty-five-minute drive up here several times a year, though, and I admit that I'll miss this place when I no longer have to come back.

I wish I could say the same about New York.

I'd give anything not to have to go back there.

As I park in the section of the campus where Maddy's room is located, I wonder if this will be one of those days when I have to go inside and look for her or whether she will come out to greet me and save us both a little time. It's not been uncommon for me to have to venture into the block where several students have their accommodation and look for my daughter amongst a sea of empty beer bottles, piles of dirty plates and crumpled clothing. There was even a shopping trolley blocking the entrance to her door once, which was unusual in itself but even more so because her room is located on the third floor. I have absolutely no idea how a group of students got a shopping trolley up so many flights of stairs, but I have the feeling that they may have put more effort into that task than some of them put into studying for their exams.

But unlike some of the other students here, like the spaced-out, long-haired young man who shuffles past my car looking like he's in need of a good night's sleep, I can't fault Maddy's work ethic. Her grades seem to have been good so far, and all indications point to her passing her degree with flying colours in just a few months' time. But as this is the first day of the Easter holidays, at least in the student world anyway, she can put away the textbooks and forget all about dissertations because it's time for her to have a break from this place, a break she deserves, though I wish she'd picked any other city on the planet to have it in.

Having got out of the car, I'm just about to go inside and try and find her when I hear the sound of suitcase wheels running over concrete. A second later, Maddy appears from around the side of the building I'm parked in front of with her luggage in tow.

'Hey! Good afternoon!' I say, pleased to see my girl for the first time in several weeks.

But Maddy does not greet me with quite the same fervour and as she gets nearer, I get some idea why. The pale face, the bags under the eyes and the energy drink bottle in her right hand are a giveaway, and it all adds up to her having had a very late night last night.

'What time did you get to bed?' I ask her as she reaches me. 'Or did you not make it that far?'

'Urghh,' Maddy groans before letting go of her suitcase and allowing me to put it in the car for her.

'Nice to see you too,' I say with a chuckle before we both get in and I start the engine. When I do, the radio automatically comes on again, but Maddy is quick to turn it off, and that tells me that a headache is just another of the symptoms to add to what is quite clearly a diagnosis of a very bad hangover. But by the time I have forced a little small talk and made it back onto the motorway, Maddy has perked up a little, a combination of the contents of the ingredients in her energy drink entering her bloodstream and also the fact she is still young, meaning recovery is much quicker at her age.

Oh, to be on the cusp of turning twenty-one again.

The next big milestone for me is the half-century.

If that's not enough to leave me feeling a little melancholy, what Maddy says next sure is. That's because she's back on her favourite topic and pretty much the only thing she has messaged home to talk about over the last few weeks.

New York.

'I've seen this really cool diner on Instagram that we have to go to for breakfast,' Maddy tells me before holding up her phone to show me a photo of it. I can't pay too much attention to her phone because I'm driving, but I give it a cursory glance and when I do, I see what looks like a classic American diner, all red seats, booths and breakfast bars, and as Maddy goes on, she tells me which block it is located on in the city.

While I don't know the diner specifically because I'm guessing it opened after we left New York, I do know the block she is referring to because there used to be a lovely Italian restaurant there where Lorna and I would go for a rare date night whenever we got a babysitter. But it was rare because Lorna was always anxious about hiring a person who was essentially a stranger to look after our children, which meant we didn't do it often. But that was the only choice for a babysitter we had because all our family was back in England, and the friends we had made in New York already had enough to do looking after their own children.

'Looks good,' I say, and I flash Maddy a smile, though the expression is a world away from how I am feeling on the inside. But my daughter has no idea that I am feeling so apprehensive about going back to New York, and why would she? She was only six when we left, and she had no idea what the real reason was for her parents suddenly deciding to move. She has asked me several times as she got older, as has Alex, but I just give them the same answer I gave to everybody else who asked, be they people in America or England.

"Given the uncertain financial climate at that time, we decided it best to return home."

That's right, I blamed our move home on the recession of 2008, which, to be fair, was a mighty good excuse because everyone in the world knew about the banking collapse and not many people could argue with it. But the truth is it was just an excuse because I left New York and brought my family home for a very different reason.

I had to escape that city.

If I had stayed, I doubt I would have gotten away with what I did there.

3

MADDY

I'm not usually thrilled about going home because I'm having such a great time as a student at uni, and I would rather be in my own space on campus than in a house with Mum and Dad. But it's different this time because I'm super excited about the trip we are about to take, and as Dad steers us off the motorway, I check the time on my phone and get a thrill when I realise that this time tomorrow, I'll finally be back in New York again.

People always think it is cool when I tell them that I spent the first six years of my life in NYC, just like they think it is very uncool when I tell them that my parents made me move back to England instead of allowing me to stay there and grow up as a cool East Coast girl.

I have to agree with them.

If only my parents had stayed in America, then my whole life would have been very different. It's not that it's been terrible in the UK, but living in the northwest of England is very different to living in New York. It's nowhere near as glitzy and glamorous here as it is over there, and I've spent many a night, particularly through my teenage years, wondering what I would have been doing if I was still in the Big Apple.

I used to watch episodes of *Sex In The City* and *Friends* and then go and moan to Mum because I could have been like the characters of Carrie Bradshaw or Rachel

Green, having a cool career in the city, going on dates with handsome men in glamorous places and generally just having lots of adventures in such a famous place. But Mum used to tell me that the New York I saw on television is very different to the one that exists in real life. She really had fuel for her argument when she found out, much to her surprise as well as mine, that most of the scenes in *Friends* were actually filmed in L.A., not New York. But I didn't care because the way I saw it, I had been robbed of the chance to have a very different life in a very unique place, and while I don't resent my parents for moving us back to England, I have always maintained that I wanted to go back there – first, for a holiday and then one day, possibly to live.

For some reason, Mum and Dad have never been too keen on that idea, and they have said that if I do want to move to an exciting new city, I should try London first because that's not as far away, and they could help me much easier there if I was to get into any difficulties. But I don't want London, I want New York, and that's why I decided on it for my twenty-first birthday present.

I know it's a very big present, and I'm extremely grateful because it must cost quite a lot of money to go there, but what was I supposed to say when Mum and Dad asked me what I wanted for my birthday? My brother is the same too. He's always wished we'd stayed in NY, though he was only three when we moved back, so I'm not sure how much he remembers of it. He pretends he can recall parts of New York from memory, but I think he's just saying that. But I genuinely can remember. I remember the house we lived in and the

25

school I went to. I also remember what it was like to look up at all those tall buildings and feel the energy from all those people rushing around below them. Even now, certain smells like popcorn or frying onions make me think of the food vendors on the corner of the busy streets or outside Yankee stadium.

I really, really can't wait to go back.

And tomorrow, I'll get my wish.

Mum's car isn't on the drive as Dad parks outside our house, and he tells me she will have gone into Manchester to collect my brother, so I guess it's just the two of us for a little while longer. But that's okay because I've always got on well with Dad, probably because I have plenty in common with him. We're both good with numbers and having seen how well a career in finance has done for him, I have chosen to go down that path too, hoping to use my impending Economics degree to eventually get myself a top job that pays well and gives me the opportunity to work abroad. Obviously, while I haven't told Mum and Dad yet, my dream is to work for a company that has offices in New York, and who knows, maybe I will fit in a little job hunting while I'm over there on holiday. That way, I could have a job lined up in NY before I even graduate. Wouldn't that be cool?

As well as having similar interests career-wise, I'm also a big sports fan like Dad. Despite him possibly wondering whether having a little girl would mean a lack of sporting activities, I spent many a happy afternoon with Dad at the park playing ball games, and I'm currently in the women's football, tennis and netball teams at uni. Our shared love of sports has given us extra bonding time, and we'll get even more of it when we're in NYC because we have tickets to a Yankees game, which I'm really excited about because I have a few memories of going to watch them when I was young, the best of which is being lifted up high into the air as Dad was celebrating a game-winning home run.

But even if we didn't have so much in common, I know I'd still be extremely close to my dad.

That's because of what he did seven years ago.

I was fourteen and Alex was eleven when we woke up one night to the smell of smoke, and as we ran from our bedrooms, we saw a raging fire at the bottom of the stairs. It was terrifying, and I'll never forget the noise of the raging inferno that seemed to be blocking our only way out of the house. But I'll also never forget what Dad did to make sure that no matter what, we all got out of there alive.

He literally ran through those flames to get Alex and me to the door, and he made sure Mum was safe too. If it hadn't been for him, then the three of us would possibly have just kept panicking and quickly succumbed to smoke inhalation, but Dad did not allow such a thing to happen, being brave and getting us out with only injuries to his body and not ours.

If I ever need a reminder of his love for me, then I only need to look at the burns on his arms whenever he is wearing a t-shirt, which is not something he does often because he's a little self-conscious about them, though he has got better about that over time. Those burns are permanent reminders of what he did to keep his loved ones safe, whenever I catch a glimpse of them like I did on the drive home today, when he turned the steering wheel and the sleeves on his jacket rose up a little.

That fire is the one blot on my childhood, the only thing that stopped it from being perfect, but it could have been so much worse, and we're all just grateful to Dad that it wasn't.

As we arrive on the driveway, I see our house through the windscreen and as always, it gives me good feelings. The only time it didn't was when the entire front of it was covered in black soot and the hallway and lounge were burnt-out shells, but it has long since been restored to looking its best again, and hopefully, it will stay this way forever. I hope Mum and Dad never sell this place because it would be nice to always have it to come back to, even if I do end up living overseas for a while, and I'd miss it if it was gone.

'I'm going to go and get my things ready,' I tell Dad after we've entered the house, and it's only a short climb up the staircase before I'm back in my old bedroom surrounded by memories of the past. Even though I've been away at uni for most of the last three years and even though my brother threatened to take ownership of it, Mum and Dad have left this room as it was before I left. That means there are still a few questionable posters on the wall featuring some of my teenage crushes, as well as a few cuddly bears from my childhood that neither I nor my parents have had the heart to throw away. I also see the painting of the Manhattan skyline that hangs above my bed, which was a present from my grandparents after I told them how much I missed New York. I'm not sure Mum and Dad appreciated them buying it for me because they didn't seem too happy about it at the time, but this is my room, so I was free to decorate it however I wanted to. But I'm focusing more on the future rather than the past now as I open my wardrobe and look inside to see if there is anything in here that I want to take with me to America.

The first thing I pull out is my trusty, white Yankees cap because I know I'll definitely want to wear that at the game we're going to, and I'll also want to take the cool Knicks hoody that I ordered online a couple of Christmases ago. There are a few other things in here that I intend to take as well, and after losing myself in the very important task of packing for my holiday, I almost get so busy that I forget to update my Instagram followers on what I'm up to.

I don't exactly have a huge following online, but there are over 1000 people who follow my account; many of them are my friends but many of them are just horny guys who follow me for any photos I put up of me and my friends on nights out. I do like to use social media a lot, so I decide to take a quick photo of my Yankees cap lying beside my suitcase before I post it, along with the caption:

Finally headed back to my roots! NYC here I come!

I'm happy with the post so I upload it and with that done, I go back to packing. But just to get me in the mood for my trip even more, I decide to play an episode of *Friends* on my phone. So what if most of the interior shots in this sitcom were filmed on the West Coast rather than the East? I'm not going to let that minor fact spoil my enjoyment of one of my favourite TV shows, and as I watch Rachel, Ross, Joey and the rest of them getting up to more silliness on my screen, I smile to myself because pretty soon, I won't have to get my fix of New York from a TV show or a painting that hangs above my bed.

I'll be there for real. Standing on the streets. Right in the middle of it all.

Happy 21st to me.

And happy 18th to my little brother, too, because I know he is just as excited about this trip as I am.

4

ALEX

It's funny because right now, I should be counting down the hours until I get on that plane to America. It's a trip I have been eager to make for several years and now I'm on the cusp of being there. But suddenly, I don't feel like I want to go and fly for almost eight hours to be in another country.

I want to stay here, and the reason I want to stay is staring me right in the face.

'Enjoy your trip, buddy. I'll see you when you get back. And text me while you're away; I want to see photos of you on Broadway!'

I smile at my excitable friend, James, the first person I got talking to when these acting classes started last week and the person whom I have become closest to out of all the other dozens of attendees here. But while I'm smiling on the outside, I'm feeling pain, confusion and despair on the inside, and that's because I have feelings for James, feelings that go well beyond what he or anyone else who knows me would expect me to be experiencing.

I wouldn't say I'm in love with him yet because I've not known him quite long enough. Oh, who am I kidding? I can't stop thinking about him even though we've only just met, and he is the reason why I would rather stay here than go to New York for the next four days.

'I will,' I tell James as he heads away - the handsome man who is totally oblivious to the fact that I am enamoured with him far beyond the point of me being his friend. He's got it all. The good looks, the great sense of humour, the kind soul and on top of that, he wants to be an actor, just like me. We share the same dream, and that only makes me feel drawn to him more.

But there is a problem, and it's quite a big one. James has a girlfriend. He's not interested in men - not in the same way as I am, anyway. Even more than that, not he nor anybody else knows what I am feeling on the inside.

As far as anyone would guess, I'm into girls too, not guys.

Not even my family know my sexuality, and I'm not sure if and when I will tell them.

I let out a sigh as I turn and walk away from the room where I've just spent the last six hours being put through various acting exercises by our teacher, Sam. He's an actor in his fifties who had a bit of a television career a couple of decades ago, starring in a few episodes of British television staples like *Casualty*, *The Bill* and 1990's soap opera, *Brookside*, although that last one was a very minor role. But while he is now seemingly resigned to teaching the next generation how to act rather than still chasing the Hollywood dream himself, I have big plans and ambitions for my future.

Or at least I did before I met James.

As I leave the college building and step out onto a busy street in the heart of Manchester, I wonder how my life could have changed so quickly. Only a week ago, before James came into it, my entire focus was on not only trying to become an actor, but on making it big in America. I've always wanted to go and work there, and even though I'm still only seventeen, I don't want the years to pass by quickly. If I'm not careful, I'll end up just like Sam before I know it, just another washed-up UK actor who nobody really recognises and who is more of a teacher than someone who stands in front of a camera or treads the boards on a big theatrical stage. But right now, my head is not filled with dizzying fantasies of starring in a Broadway play in New York or becoming the breakout star of a big-budget movie filmed in a studio in Los Angeles. Instead, it is filled with thoughts of James and how I'm going to miss him terribly until the next time I can see him again.

Spotting Mum's car parked amongst the several that have ignored the double yellow lines on the road, I rush to the vehicle and get in so we can be on our way quickly.

'Hey, love! How was class today?' Mum asks chirpily, totally unaware that my heart is aching terribly for a guy she doesn't even know exists.

'Good,' I say quietly as we drive away, and when we join the traffic queuing at the red light, I think about how my life so far feels like one big series of red lights too.

From being rejected from numerous auditions ever since I started trying to be an actor at the age of twelve to going through most of my teenage years failing to persuade my parents to take me back to America because I felt I'd like it there more than here, I'm used to hearing the word no, which is effectively another version of a red light. Now, as I sit here in this car and stare at that glowing red circle that we need to turn green before we can proceed, I feel like I am faced with yet another frustrating situation in which I can't possibly get what I want.

I'll never be with James, not how I want to be anyway, because even if he knew how I felt, he wouldn't be interested. But he doesn't know - nobody does - because just like with James or any of the other guys I've had a crush on over the last few years, I've never told a single person.

It's weird to keep such a secret from my family but as far as they all know, I'm just a regular young man who will get a girlfriend one day, get married to her and have kids.

I wonder what they would say if they knew the truth?

They'd all be shocked, Dad especially. I guess they'd still love me and say it didn't bother them, and Mum and Maddy would probably mean it, but would Dad? I've always thought that he might be disappointed in me, even though he's never actually said so. It's just that after having a girl, I'm sure he was excited when he found out his second child was to be a boy because then it meant he would get to do all the father-son activities.

Dad is sports mad, so he must have dreamt about taking me to games with him, as well as the pair of us playing with the balls in the garden and having debates about our favourite teams and players. But I'm very different to Dad in more ways than one. I hate sport, despite him trying his best to get me to love it as much as he does. He even named me after a baseball player, a fact my sister told me one day and a fact that surprised me because I can't think of anything more boring than a game of baseball.

While I like performing, I much prefer to do it on a stage rather than a field, and whatever gene he has that makes him love sports, I certainly didn't inherit it. But my sister did. She has always been a bit of a tom-boy, and while she still does a few more typically girly things with Mum, she watches football games on TV with Dad and likes going to matches with him. That's why I've always felt like she is closer to him than I am. I feel distant from Dad, even though I know he loves me and just wants me to be happy. It's just that we've always found it harder to relate to each other than anyone else, and that's why the thought of him finding out that I'd rather marry a man than a woman makes me fear it might be the thing that really makes him wish I was more like him.

'So Maddy's home now,' Mum tells me as we drive on again. 'Your father picked her up earlier.'

'Cool,' I mutter, but while normally I'd be thrilled to have my sister home again because I miss her when she's away, I just feel deflated today. Unfortunately, Mum notices.

'Hey, what's wrong? We're going to New York tomorrow, or have you forgotten?' she asks me with a confused smirk. 'You know, the place you've been pestering me about going back to for God knows how many years.'

Mum's not wrong there. I have been pestering her about a return to NYC for a long time because even though I can't remember much about living there, I pretend like I do and therefore, can pretend like my life would be a million times better if we were still there now. Maybe if we'd stayed there, then I'd have already had my big break in acting and have been a child star with multiple film and TV credits to my name. There is certainly more of a vibrant acting scene in New York than there is in Manchester, that's for sure. But that's not the only reason why I wish we'd stayed there instead of moving here. It's also because I wonder if my life would be easier in terms of my sexuality. Maybe I would have found it easier to come out there, or maybe I might not even need to at all. What if staying there might have meant I was attracted to women rather than men?

I know that last thought is a stupid one because I doubt where I lived would have had much of an impact on my innate sexuality, but I've still thought it and believed it several times in my past. That's why, to me, New York has always been this place where I felt I might find a little salvation, as if going back there would reset me and make my life easier. It's also why I, along with my sister, have spent so many years begging Mum and Dad to take us back there, as if they robbed us of some future we never got to experience simply by bringing us back to England when we were too small to have a say in it. But now I'm getting my wish, and we're going to NY tomorrow.

So why am I still unhappy?

'I'm just tired,' I tell Mum by way of an explanation as to why I'm not super excited. 'Tough class today.'

'I see. Well, make sure you have an early night tonight,' Mum advises me as she continues to steer us out of the busy city and back to the quieter suburbs where we reside. 'Remember the taxi to the airport is picking us up at four-thirty in the morning, so it's a very early start. Get packing as soon as you get in and then straight to bed.'

'Mum, I'm not a kid,' I moan, wishing she'd talk to me more like the adult I have become.

'I know you're not. I'm just saying,' she replies before smiling at me to let me know that she didn't mean to annoy me. But she has annoyed me, just like everything else in my life is annoying me at the moment.

I'm annoyed that I'm not going to see James for a while. I'm annoyed that he has no idea how I feel about him because I'm too scared to tell him. And most of all, I'm annoyed that this upcoming trip to New York might not be the life-changing experience I have been expecting it to be.

But little did I know, I was definitely wrong about that last part.

5

LORNA

After a typically eventful day in the life of my family, it was almost midnight by the time I'd finished packing my things for our holiday. While staying up so late would not usually bother me because I've always been somewhat of a night owl, it's hardly ideal when I know my alarm is going to go off in three hours, and the taxi for the airport will be outside an hour after that.

As I collapse into bed beside my husband, who put his own head down on his pillow half an hour ago, I wonder if he might already be asleep. But I get my answer when he rolls over and puts his arm around my waist before giving me a kiss on my bare shoulder.

'Sorry. I thought you might be sleeping,' I say quietly, my voice a whisper because I know, or at least hope, that Maddy and Alex are asleep in their bedrooms nearby.

'It's kind of hard to sleep when my wife is huffing and puffing as she packs a suitcase in the same room as me,' Jack replies with a chuckle, and now I feel bad because I obviously wasn't being as quiet with the packing as I was trying to be.

'I'm sorry,' I say while wondering how the pair of us are going to be able to function soon on such little sleep. But it becomes clear that it's not just the busy day and the late night packing that is contributing to our lack of rest.

'How are you feeling?' Jack asks me, and while that could be a very general question, I know exactly what he is referring to.

'Anxious,' I reply honestly.

'It'll be okay.'

'Will it?'

'Yes, of course. It's been a long time. If anything was going to happen, then it would have happened by now.'

I guess Jack is right but despite his trying to reassure me, I still feel unsettled because deep down, I know something is wrong and no amount of time passing will ever change that. It's like going to a doctor when you feel something changing in your body. Even if all the tests come back clear, nobody knows your body better than you do, and if you still think something might be wrong, it could just be that the problem is not advanced enough yet to be picked up on any scan or blood sample. It's the same with what Jack and I did in New York in 2008. I don't care that fifteen years have gone by since because that doesn't change it or make it better, not when we know there is still something very wrong. Just because the police haven't been to our door since that fateful year, it doesn't mean we should essentially return to the scene of the crime and tempt fate.

'I really wish we'd just been firmer and said no,' I tell Jack as we continue to both lie wide awake in the darkness and feel the dread that comes with knowing our flight back to that city is getting closer by the minute.

'Did we have to give in? We should have just said we couldn't afford it, and they might have dropped it.'

'This is Maddy and Alex we're talking about,' Jack replies in a hushed tone as he strokes my hair and does a somewhat small but insignificant job of making me feel a tiny bit better under the circumstances. 'They would never have dropped it. It was either we go back there with them or they go alone, and I know I'd rather be there just to make sure they are okay. It's a big city and a dangerous one if people aren't careful.'

'People like us?'

Jack doesn't need to answer that one because we both know the truth there.

'Try and get some sleep,' he tells me before giving me another kiss and then rolling over, leaving me alone on my side of the bed to try and follow his advice. But if I do get any sleep over the next few hours, then it is just ten minutes here and there, and by the time my alarm goes off, I am utterly exhausted. But despite that, I have the feeling that it was far better to be awake for most of the night than to fall into a deep sleep because that might have been where the nightmares could have started.

The last thing I needed was to see New York in my dreams before I get to see it in real life.

By the time the taxi arrived, I didn't have much time to think about much else other than making sure everybody was ready to leave the house, and despite it being organised chaos, all four of us somehow got our luggage into the waiting vehicle and were strapped into our seats without too much delay. Then it was off to the airport for our 8am flight, and while the drive there was made in darkness, the sun was coming up by the time we had dropped our luggage, picked up our boarding passes and made it through the security checkpoints.

The sight of the clear blue sky on the other side of the large windows of the airport terminal went a little way to making me feel a bit better, as did the hearty breakfast and two cups of coffee I had at the restaurant that was full of other Brits who were all due to jet off on their holidays over the next couple of hours. Jack seemed in better spirits than last night too, wolfing down a big plate of bacon, sausages and beans while finding time to chat to Maddy about last night's baseball scores and also ask Alex what he planned to do to kill time during our seven-hour flight.

Our son told him that he would be watching movies, which was hardly a surprise because he loves films, and as we left our table and headed for our departure gate, I was hoping I would be able to find a movie or two of my own on the in-flight entertainment that might make the journey a little more enjoyable. But despite feeling like I am in quite an optimistic mood after breakfast, that all changes quickly when an airline employee's voice comes over the tannoy to tell all passengers of Flight BZ-172 that they can begin boarding now.

My stomach lurches and my hands start sweating as my heartbeat quickens and my mouth goes dry, but I guess nobody else in my family notices those things because they all stand up and collect their carry-on bags before following the orders of the airline staff.

But I'm still sitting in my seat, and it's only when Jack looks back and notices me does he realise I am struggling.

'Let's go,' he says to me quietly as Maddy and Alex march ahead of us, and my husband offers me his hand to help me up. But when I take it, he realises how sweaty my palms are, something he surely wasn't expecting and something that is a strong sign that I am way more nervous than he realised.

'It'll be okay, I promise,' he tells me, but it sounded a little forced when he said that as if he is trying to convince himself of that fact as well as me.

'You mean it?' I ask him, hating that I need to seek further reassurance, but I'm feeling so weak that I need all the help I can get.

'Yes, I do,' Jack says with a smile, and as I stand up, I take a deep breath and force myself to forge on. I just need to get in the queue, hand over my passport, smile at the person who checks it and then get on the plane. Then all I have to do is strap myself into my seat, and we'll be gone. The next four days will fly by in no time, and I'll be back in England before I know it, wondering what I was so worried about. Not only that, but Maddy and Alex will have had the best time of their lives and be so grateful to me and their father for giving them such a lavish birthday present that they will never forget. I am doing this for my children, and I keep that at the forefront of my mind as I take my place in the queue behind them and beside my husband.

But despite being well aware that I am doing this for them, it doesn't soothe me quite as much as it should.

That's because I've done lots of things in my life that have been for my children and not all of them can be considered good.

I'm going back to New York for them, but they are also the reason I left that city.

I couldn't risk losing them, but to stay there would have meant increasing the chances of me and Jack being torn away from them. Moving back reduced those chances, and fortunately, my family has stayed intact ever since.

But will it still be intact by the end of this trip?

Or are all my worst nightmares finally about to come true?

6

JACK

I've made this journey many times before, flying along this exact route over the Atlantic Ocean. I've sat on many a plane just like this one and stared out of the window at the tip of the wing cutting through the clear blue sky, and I've enjoyed my fair share of snacks from the trolley that the cabin crew wheeled past my seat from time to time. I know what it's like to see the colours below my window go from the green fields of Ireland to the blue expanse of the Atlantic Ocean and, finally, to the steel and concrete grey of New York, and I have spent many a moment looking down at what lies several miles beneath the cabin and marvelling at the beauty of it all. I've also watched my fair share of movies at 38,000ft, as well as read plenty of books and flicked through the pages of dozens of glossy magazines as I passed the seven hours, fifty minute flight time as best I could.

But never have I ever done it all with such a knot in my stomach and sense of impending doom hanging over me like I have now.

'Nervous flyer?'

The question is directed at me and comes from the elderly man who is getting back into his seat in front of me after he got up to make the short trip to the restroom. I guess this guy has noticed how apprehensively I have been staring out of the window and assumes I am just somebody who gets anxious when I take to the skies. I'm also guessing he is a New York native because he speaks with a heavy Brooklyn accent.

'Oh, no. I'm fine,' I tell him with an awkward smile, but he doesn't look like he believes that.

'My daughter used to get nervous when she went on planes but as I always reminded her, this is the safest form of travel,' the man says with a kind smile. 'You are much better being up here than down there on all those busy roads or whizzing around on those overcrowded trains.'

'Sure,' I say, nodding my head and letting the man know that he has successfully reassured me and can leave me in peace now. But he doesn't do that. Instead, he puts his arms on the top of his seat and leans forward a little before asking me if it will be my first time visiting New York.

'No. I used to work there,' I tell him before glancing at Maddy sitting beside me and Alex sitting on the other side of her. But neither of them are paying attention to my conversation because they both have their headphones on and are watching a movie on the in-flight entertainment. As for Lorna, she is sitting across the aisle and while I see that she is looking at me, I give her a small smile to show that I'm fine, and she goes back to reading her book again.

'Oh, wow. What did you do for work?' comes the next question from the well-meaning but nosy passenger.

'I worked for a bank.'

'Ahh, I should have guessed. It had to be something to do with finance. My son works in Manhattan, and he tells me his workplace is full of Brits. I guess you all come over to chase the American dream, hey?'

I force a smile as he chuckles to himself.

'So how did that work out for you?' he asks me then.

'Excuse me?'

'The American dream. Did you find it? Or did you go back home to England thinking it was all just an illusion?'

'Oh, erm. No, it was great. I just moved back for family reasons.'

'I see,' the man says before casting his eyes over the two people sitting beside me. 'These your kids?'

'Yep.'

'You're a lucky man.'

The man smiles at me one more time before retaking his seat and going back to minding his own business, but even though he has finally left me alone, I keep replaying the last thing he said over and over again in my mind.

I'm a lucky man.

If only he knew just what kind of luck I've had in my life, then he wouldn't have made such a throwaway remark. That's because I know exactly what it is like to be in the wrong place at the wrong time, and I certainly know what it is like to curse my luck and feel like I'm doomed. But on the other hand, I suppose I have to have had some good luck in my life otherwise I wouldn't have managed to make it this long without suffering the consequences of the bad fortune I endured. Either way, call me anything.

But lucky, I am most certainly not.

Alone again with my thoughts, I remind myself of my plan for this flight. I intend to spend the majority of this journey taking advantage of the free drinks included in the price of my ticket, and when I see a member of the cabin crew passing down the aisle, I signal to them to let them know I'm ready for another can of lager. This will be my third since take-off, but who's counting? Besides, I'm on holiday. But as Lorna watches me accepting the new can and observes me pouring its contents into a small plastic cup, she gives me a look that lets me know she is aware that my indulging in alcohol on this plane has nothing to do with me being in the holiday mood.

The reason we are sitting apart rather than next to each other is because Maddy and Alex wanted to sit beside each other so they could chat, and that meant Lorna and I would have to split because there are only three seats together. But we'll all be moving around and sitting in various seats throughout the flight, taking multiple chances to get up and stretch our legs, although Lorna told me as we boarded this plane that the one seat she did not want to sit in was the one by the window. She's never liked to see outside the plane in all the years I've known her because she always worries that she will see something that will scare her, like the engine catching fire or the wing breaking off. At one point, I was worried her anxiety over flying might be the thing that ruined the chances of me accepting the offer to go and work in America, but Lorna said she was okay to get on a plane as long as she didn't have to see how high up she was while on it.

I smile at my wife and raise my plastic cup to her when I see her look at me again, as if to say 'cheers' before I drink. I'm pleased when she smiles back, and she does look a little more relaxed than she did back at the gate when I thought she appeared on the verge of a nervous breakdown. It's a far cry from how she was the first time we made this flight together after we had sold our home in England and embarked on an adventure with a very little Maddy in tow.

My heart aches for that simpler time, a time when I had everything to look forward to. A new job, a new city to live in, a new baby to help nurture. I didn't realise it then but things really were perfect. But that's the problem with a heavy conscience. You don't appreciate how peaceful life was before you had something to feel guilty about and by the time you do, it is too late to ever go back to how you were before.

The beer helps improve my mood, though, as does the next one I enjoy forty minutes later, and after watching an action movie that I missed when it was showing at the cinema a few months ago, I'm feeling quite comfortable. I notice that Maddy must be too because she is having a nap, and I smile at my daughter, who is certainly much bigger than she was the last time I flew to New York with her. She is much quieter too because from what I recall, she spent at least half that last flight crying, and landing was a nightmare because the change in cabin pressure played havoc with her little ears. But she's not so little anymore, and the days of tears and tantrums are over, or at least they are unless she ends up having her heart broken by a boy at some point, which has been known to happen on occasion.

For now, she is peaceful, and I keep smiling as I gaze at Alex too. My son is lost in some movie, his full attention on the tiny screen on the back of the seat in front of him, and I wouldn't expect anything less because he has always been enamoured with watching actors at work. Some people his age have the attention span of a goldfish and wouldn't be able to watch a whole film without checking their phone dozens of times, but Alex has always given the performers on screen his full attention. I guess that's because he's not just watching them for entertainment but for learning purposes too. He's studying them all and hoping to pick up tips and tricks that could help him with his own acting so that one day, he might be lucky enough to star in a movie that others will watch intently.

I'm proud of my son and his lofty dreams, though I'd be lying if I said things had always been easy between us. I'm much more comfortable hanging out with Maddy because we share many of the same interests, whereas I've always felt things were a little clunkier between Alex and me. I don't love him any less than my daughter, I just find it a little harder to relate to him sometimes, but I'm hoping that we can have a great time together on this trip. Just like Maddy, he has grown up unbelievably fast, and pretty soon, he will be spending a lot less time at home and will be disappearing into the world to find his own path, much like Maddy has already started to find her own. Then again, I doubt there'll ever be a time when either one of them doesn't phone me and tell me they need some quick cash to pay for something they can't afford.

While I've worked in numerous banks over my career, I've realised that the only one that will never go out of demand is the bank of Mum and Dad.

Like my son is doing, I decide to try and lose myself in another film, and it certainly does the trick because another couple of hours go by, and before I know it, the captain has come over the intercom and is telling us that we will shortly be making our descent into New York.

My eyes meet Lorna's and I mouth to her the words 'It'll be okay', which is something I've said to her numerous times since we booked this trip, and I'm sure it is something I'll have to keep saying to her until we are boarding the plane to fly back. Then I make a very quick dash to the toilets before switching seats with Alex so he can sit by the window because as he has reminded us, he was the youngest when we left New York so he remembers it the least and therefore, deserves to see it 'first'.

That's fine by me.

I'll put off seeing it for as long as I can.

The tray tables go up and the cabin crew make their final checks on everyone's seat belts before the plane descends fairly rapidly, and as we come down from the heavens and approach New York, I'm not sure if the lurching sensation I feel in my stomach is caused by the loss of altitude or my overall nervousness.

'I can see the Empire State!' Alex cries excitedly, and a few people seated near us giggle at that excited declaration, while Maddy leans across her brother's seat and tries to get a good look too. But I keep my eyes away from the windows, as does Lorna, because we've both seen this city plenty of times before. The office I used to work in had a spectacular view over Manhattan, and I spent many a minute wiling away time wistfully staring out at all the spectacular structures and wondering how the construction workers had been able to build them so high up into the sky. But then the plane banks to the right and despite not being eager to catch another glimpse of all those buildings again, I can't help but turn my head and look out the window and when I do, I see rows and rows of towering monuments to capitalism and wealth. Then I hear the wheels emerging from underneath the plane, and a few moments later, we make contact with the runway, the cabin juddering a little before the pilot slows us down and the plane completes its successful landing.

As Maddy and Alex keep looking out of the window and several people around the plane talk excitedly about the first thing they are going to do now they are here, Lorna and I share a knowing look.

It's a look that says both of us cannot wait to be on the plane home again.

7

LORNA

Everything I remember about this crazy place is passing by on the other side of my taxi's window as we move through the streets on our way from the airport to the hotel. The crowded sidewalks. The steam from below the surface. The noisy fire trucks. The street performers and the tourists who watch them. The long queue for half-price, last-minute tickets to a Broadway show. The sun glinting against the side of metallic buildings. The never-ending flow of yellow cabs that seem to come from all directions.

But it's not just what you can see and hear in this city, but what it makes you feel. The energy. The ambition. The potential. But even with all that and despite being surrounded by millions and millions of people, there is a strange sense that this place can be incredibly lonely because a person can easily fade into the background of such a fast-paced, cut-throat environment. I certainly had plenty of days when I felt lonely here in the past, even after I'd been in New York for a while and made new friends and found my way around. There's simply too much going on here all the time, and after the adrenaline rush of a journey into Midtown Manhattan had worn off, I often felt totally drained in a way that I never felt back home.

'This is amazing,' Maddy says as she stares out of her window and gawks at all the sights she is seeing for the first time as an adult. Alex is also taking it all in in a state of awe. But this is nothing new to Jack and me, though it once was, so we can appreciate how exhilarating this is for our kids.

I'm shocked a moment later when we drive past a store that I used to go in years ago to buy children's clothes, and the fact it is still here is both comforting and stressful.

Comforting because it's familiar.

Stressful because I don't want things to be the same as they were when I was last here.

I want things to have changed. Progressed. Moved on. And I want the past to have been forgotten, or if not forgotten, at least feel such a long time ago that nothing can be done about it. But then I see a few more places I remember, from certain restaurants and coffee shops to other stores too, and while there are plenty of new things lining the sidewalk, there are lots of blasts from the past as well.

Fifteen years is a long time.

But maybe not long enough.

I turn away from the window then, wishing to have a brief respite from looking out at the city, and when I do, I see Maddy holding up her phone, seemingly capturing everything that is passing us by.

'What are you doing?' I ask her, suddenly feeling very anxious.

'Just filming a video,' she replies, keeping her phone to the glass.

'What for?'

'My Instagram.'

I feel a shiver down my spine then, and while Maddy can never understand the real reason why I am about to ask her to do a certain thing, it is imperative that she listens to me and obeys me.

'Don't be putting any photos or videos up online,' I tell her, an instruction she looks absolutely mortified at.

'What are you talking about?' she asks me, her phone still recording.

'You can do it when we get home.'

'Are you serious?'

'Yes, I am.'

Jack glances back at me then from his position in the front seat beside the driver, and he must know why I have just told Maddy what I have. But he doesn't pass comment, leaving me to fight this battle alone.

'Mum, are you joking? I'm not going to come to New York and stay off social media! I want my friends to see what I'm doing!'

'They can see when you get back. I mean it, Maddy; I don't want you on your phone for the whole of this trip. Your father and I have spent a lot of money, and it would be nice if you were present with us while we are here. The same goes for you as well, Alex. No pictures on Instagram or TikTok or whatever you use these days.'

Maddy looks at me like I have lost my mind, while Alex looks confused too, and I am aware that telling my social-media-obsessed children to not use social media while they are in New York seems absurd. But I've just given them a reason that might make my request seem a little more understandable. I've told them it's because their parents didn't bring them here so they could stare at their phones the whole time. We came here for quality family time, to celebrate their upcoming birthdays, and they should appreciate what we have done for them rather than bury their heads in their phones instead of talking to us.

But it's a tough sell, not least because the reason I just gave is complete nonsense. I don't realistically expect my children to stay off their phones while they are here, but I'm going to try and get them to at least not share every little part of their trip online because the truth is I am worried.

I am worried about who might see that they are here.

The mistake Jack and I made just before we left this city, the one that has haunted the pair of us ever since, was not something that could easily be forgotten by those affected by it. While the wounds may no longer be raw, they still run deep and, ultimately, are the kind a person never fully recovers from, and that is why I'm so anxious now about any of my children loudly announcing their arrival in this city for all of social media to see. I'd prefer it if we were discreet while we were here, slipping in and out of the city for a short, enjoyable stay. Minimal attention. Minimal fuss. Nobody but us has to know we are here. But I can't explicitly explain that to Maddy or Alex without tipping them off to the fact that their parents did something bad here, so I just have to try and make my point under the guise of me wanting my kids to be more 'present.'

I'll need all the luck I can get with that.

Thankfully, Maddy puts away her phone, and while it might only be a victory in the short term, it'll do for now. A moment later and our taxi comes to a stop outside our hotel, and as Jack deals with giving the driver a tip, I step out onto the busy sidewalk and soak up the sounds, sights and smells of this bustling metropolis. But while it's familiar to me, Maddy and Alex are experiencing it all for the first time, and the pair of them excitedly point out things to each other while I focus more on getting our luggage out of the taxi and into this hotel. Fortunately, a bellhop appears to give me some assistance and after he has put our suitcases onto a trolley, the four of us follow him into a very spacious lobby, where we are led to the front desk to check in.

I quickly run through our details with the kind woman on reception before we are furnished with the keys to the two rooms we have booked here. Jack and I have a double room, and Maddy and Alex are sharing a twin, something that the pair of them grumbled about initially before I told them that they should be grateful for what they have because this hotel was not cheap. I also reminded them that their sharing a room would mean money was saved for far more exciting things during our trip, like meals and tickets, so that got them to stop moaning and appreciate that sharing a room was actually a sensible idea. Besides, we're hardly going to be in our rooms much anyway because nobody comes to a place like this to lie on their bed and watch cable TV. We'll be out exploring and seeing everything this famous city has to offer, and as the four of us enter the elevator with the bellhop and our luggage accompanying us too, Maddy and Alex are chattering about what they want to do first.

As the elevator ascends, taking us up to the eighteenth floor, I'm reminded of how everything in this city seems to exist at height. Be it a hotel room, an apartment, a doctor's office or even just a shopping mall, it feels like everything is high above the ground. This is certainly no place for a person with a fear of elevators, that's for sure. We arrive on the eighteenth floor in the blink of an eye, and after we have been shown to our rooms, the bellhop gratefully accepts a few dollars from Jack's wallet before leaving us alone. Then, as the kids enter their room, Jack and I go into ours, and after a long journey and weeks of stress leading up to this moment for various reasons, it is a relief to see that the room is absolutely perfect.

A huge double bed surrounded by lots of carpet space, a big wardrobe and sizeable mini-bar and a spacious bathroom with a walk-in shower means the pair of us will be very comfortable while we are here, and as Jack falls back onto the bed, he lets out an almighty sigh. That tells me he is glad the travelling portion of our trip is over with now, at least until we go and do it all again the other way around in a few days. But I've not quite decompressed yet, and I find myself going over to the window and looking outside just to see what I can spot. To anybody else, it would look like I am checking out the view from my room, but I've not gone to the window to look out at all the other tall buildings or gaze down at the tops of the cars on the road or the tiny, almost ant-sized humans walking way down below. I've gone to look out because even though we're high up and it seems ridiculous to think it, I'm checking for one thing, and it's not to watch other people.

It's to see if anybody is watching us.

8

JACK

Just as I told my wife several times before we got here, everything will be okay.

And so far, it's been more than that.

It's been great.

Our first afternoon and evening in New York flew by in a whirlwind of bright lights and big meals. Maddy and Alex had been desperate to see Times Square, so we went there first, and Lorna and I shared a smile as our children marvelled at all the giant screens and huge billboards that surrounded them. It was a nice moment between my wife and me because this trip was all about making our children happy, and despite any misgivings we had about being where we were, we knew in that moment that it would have been wrong to deprive them of this experience just because of our own fears and worries. After that, we tucked into the first, but not the last, big meal of the holiday, enjoying burgers, fries and copious amounts of cola at a very busy and very loud restaurant with American flags hanging from the rafters and framed photos of iconic US celebrities all over the walls.

Our first day in NY concluded with us visiting a couple of department stores, where Maddy bought a baseball cap while Alex was treated to a pair of trainers, or sneakers as they call them here, with a price tag that made my eyes water slightly. But as Lorna and I kept reminding them – 'This is for your birthday so get what you want now because this is your present. There won't be anything else nearer the time.' It was important to remind our children of that so that they aren't asking questions when their actual birth dates arrive and they have nothing to unwrap.

As Lorna and I fell into bed that night, very tired, not just from the exertions of the day, but because our body clocks were off kilter and it was the middle of the night back in the UK, I once again told my wife that everything was okay. And miraculously, this time, she genuinely seemed to believe me. I know that because she slept like a baby, and by the time we got up to start our second day, Lorna was in a much better mood than she had been when we woke up in England yesterday. She was much chattier with me and also less hard on Maddy and Alex, her paranoia seemingly having subsided somewhat, leaving her loosened up enough to enjoy this experience.

Day two began with a boat ride to see the Statue of Liberty, and while the wind that blew in our faces was freezing as we cut through the water, the views of the iconic sculpture were very special, and the four of us featured in many photos that I know Lorna and I will treasure forever. From there, we paid a sombre visit to One World Trade Centre, formerly known as Freedom Tower and the site of the former World Trade Towers. While Lorna and I had just missed being here during the dreadful events of that late summer's day in September 2001, we had felt the consequences of it in the years after. I'll never forget sitting in a meeting on one of the upper floors of a downtown Manhattan skyscraper and seeing the sheer terror on the face of one of my colleagues when the fire alarm went off unexpectedly. While I was preparing to stand and calmly make my way out of the room, he ran as if his life depended on it, and it was only after speaking to somebody else in that meeting that I understood it was because he had experienced a narrow escape on that fateful day a couple of years earlier and clearly still struggled when unexpected things happened in tall towers. I also remember seeing the nervous looks on people's faces as they looked to the skies whenever they heard an aircraft flying low over the city and could only imagine how many of them had seen some terrible things that day too. That was why I made sure Maddy and Alex visited the site and paid their respects before we moved on to our next activity.

The Empire State Building was our next port of call, and after making it all the way to the observation deck on the 86th floor, the four of us marvelled at the stunning and slightly dizzying view of the city from our very high vantage point. It wasn't my first time up the Empire State, but seeing such a sight never gets old, and there was also time for a quiet moment with Lorna while Maddy and Alex were busy taking photos. I told my wife that I was glad we were making another good memory in this city to go with all the other good ones we had made here, and the implication was that one negative memory shouldn't overpower all those positive ones.

I'm not sure Lorna fully agreed with being able to cancel out the bad memory entirely, but she did agree that this place would always be part of our family's history, and it was nice that we got to experience it one more time before our kids fully grew up and flew the nest for good. After that, we managed to fit in one more very large meal that added a couple of extra inches to all of our waistlines before it was time for our group to separate for our second evening in the city.

I was taking Maddy out of Manhattan and into the Bronx, another one of the five boroughs, to where Yankee Stadium was located. While we would be enjoying a baseball game tonight, Lorna and Alex would be taking in a Broadway show, and with everybody suitably looking forward to their evening's entertainment, we said our goodbyes and split up.

As Maddy and I go underground and get on the subway, each of us wearing a different coloured Yankee cap and chattering about some of the players we will see in action tonight, I suddenly get the strangest sensation. I don't know why but for some reason, I feel like the four of us breaking off into two groups of two is a bad idea, and Maddy notices my hesitation as I look back to the open doors of the train carriage just before they close.

'Everything okay, Dad?' Maddy asks me, which makes a big change from me checking on her all the time, but I don't answer her quickly because I'm not quite sure if it is yet.

That was weird, I think to myself as the train starts moving, and we begin our journey below the city streets. *I have no idea why I just felt as bad as I did.*

Telling myself it was nothing, I smile at my daughter before picking up the baseball-themed conversation where we left off, but while we keep talking and the train gets busier at each stop as more and more Yankee fans pile into the carriage, I still feel unsettled. But it doesn't make sense because nothing has happened since we have been in New York to make me wary. Everything has gone to plan, and as far as I know, everything should continue to do so until we board our plane back home.

Maddy seems to realise that I'm not in the mood for chatting at the moment because she gives up trying to talk to me and takes out her phone, and I watch as she scrolls through several of the photos she has taken since she got here. As far as I know, she has listened to her mother's request and not posted multiple updates of the trip on her social media accounts, although neither of us have the apps that our children do on their phones, so we would have no idea what they were posting anyway. But as the train reaches its destination and we join the hordes of fans spilling out of the subway station and into the Bronx, Maddy captures a photo of the imposing stadium ahead of us, complete with the floodlights above it and the thousands of New Yorkers and tourists pouring into it.

'This has to go on Instagram,' she tells me as she shows me the photo she just took, and I have to give her credit because she has captured a brilliant image, one that I almost feel like I would like printing off and hanging in a frame in my study at home because for a big sports fan like me, it's the kind of image I'd enjoy looking at all the time. But while I'm not going to be as harsh or paranoid as her mum and tell her not to post anything online that lets others know we are here, I do still feel strangely nervous as we move through the busy crowd on the way into the stadium.

Looking around at the multitude of faces that surround me, I still can't explain my uneasiness. It's not as if I don't like crowds, and I've been to a Yankee's game before, so it's all quite familiar to me. But something is bugging me, though I'm still not quite sure what it is.

I'm just considering taking out my phone and texting Lorna to ask if she and Alex are okay but before I can do that, Maddy stops walking beside me and has a very confused look on her face as she stares at her phone.

'What is it?' I ask her as I step to the side, getting out of the flow of baseball fans streaming past us.

'I've just got a weird message on Instagram,' Maddy says with a frown on her face.

'From who?'

'I don't know. The account doesn't have a real name on it, and there's no photo either.'

'What does it say?'

I hope you are enjoying your time in New York. Make sure to stay safe. It's a big city. You don't want to get lost,' Maddy says, reading out the message.

Now it's my turn to frown, and I ask to see my daughter's phone so I can have a proper look at the message myself. Surprisingly, she hands it to me quickly, which suggests she must be a little disturbed by it because she would never normally willingly hand me her precious device but now she has, I can read the message for myself. Sure enough, it says exactly what Maddy said it did. But there's no context to it, and without knowing exactly who it came from, it's hard to really know what it means.

Is it just some random person sending a weird message, something that probably happens all the time on the internet and on social media in general?

Or is it an actual warning?

'It's weird,' Maddy says, stating the obvious before she gestures for me to give her back her phone. But before I hand it over, I click on the profile of the person who sent it. But like Maddy says, there is no photo or real name. The account is in the name of *NewYorker7823*, which doesn't tell us much, but I do discern one thing from looking at the profile. There are no posts or photos on the account, and this person has no followers, which suggests it is either a new account or one that does not get used very often. But I notice the account does follow two others, so I click on them to find out who they are. When I do, this gets more confusing.

They only follow Maddy and Alex.

'Who is this?' I ask my daughter as she snatches her phone back from me after I've failed to hand it over quickly enough.

'I don't know. Some weirdo probably,' Maddy replies. 'I'm not replying to them.'

I watch as she does something else on her phone and when I ask her what it is, she tells me she is posting the image she just took of Yankee Stadium. But now I'm not so sure that is a good idea.

That's because I don't know who that person is who just messaged her or why they only seem to follow my children's accounts.

More importantly, I don't know why they have just told Maddy to be careful about not getting lost here.

9

LORNA

There's a hum of anticipation around the large auditorium that Alex and I are currently sitting in alongside a thousand other theatre lovers. We're all here because we have tickets to watch a performance of *The Phantom of the Opera*, and as we wait for the lights to go down and the show to begin, I'm feeling pleased that the person sitting beside me seems to be happy.

Alex has been looking forward to this show ever since we booked tickets online a month ago, and he's currently reading through the brochure I bought him after we had entered the theatre, the one that features interviews with some of the cast members of this particular show as well as some facts and figures about the longevity of it and how it has been one of the most watched shows on Broadway. While he's busy reading, I'm looking at the large stage in front of us and wondering if the performers backstage are feeling nervous about coming out here soon to recite their lines.

I find it slightly puzzling that my son wishes to pursue a career in which he would be required to go on stage or in front of a camera and perform a multitude of lines he has memorised to a large audience. That's because I can't think of a more daunting way to make a living. I can safely say that I have never felt a desire to go from being a member of the watching public to being front and centre on a stage, screen or any other type of platform for that matter and if forced to, I'd be a jabbering mess who would freeze under the spotlight and forget what I was supposed to say. But my son is clearly much braver than I am because his dream is to one day be a professional in an environment like this one, to walk out and receive the adulation of a crowd and entertain each and every one of the people who have paid good money to see him and his fellow actors in full flow.

It's a tough career choice but a very brave and inspiring one, and I have no doubts that Alex can achieve all of his dreams if he puts his mind to it and never gives up. When he does, I'll make sure I am right there on the front row to witness his dreams coming true and show my support, though I will have to draw the line at him inviting me up onto the stage alongside him if he ever tried to do so because there's no chance of that happening. But he is under very strict instructions to give me a shout-out if he ends up winning a Tony Award or an Oscar one day, just like he is to invite me as his 'plus one' to any glitzy red-carpet events. That is as much of the limelight as I shall ask for.

While my son and I are here in the warmth of this theatre, Jack and Maddy are across the city, possibly shivering a little as they watch a baseball game in an outdoor stadium, and I check my phone to see if either of them has been in contact with me since we separated. But they haven't, although I see Maddy has been keen to make contact with somebody since I last saw her when Alex shows me his phone a moment later.

Looking at the screen, I see what I assume is Maddy's Instagram account and when I do, I see a photo of a stadium which I guess is where she is right now.

'Looks like somebody ignored your rule while we were here,' Alex says with a sly grin on his face, no doubt because he can't resist an opportunity to possibly get his big sister into trouble. Old habits die hard, just like sibling rivalry.

'Looks like it,' I say when I see that the stadium is the home of the New York Yankees, which means she has posted exactly where she is tonight to all her followers online. But as Jack has kept telling me, everything is okay, and so far, he has been right, so I will try not to worry and not let any of my mostly unsubstantiated fears ruin my evening.

So far, this holiday has been great. Maddy and Alex are having a good time, and that's all we came here for, so I can't have too many regrets. As the lights go down in the theatre and Alex puts his phone away to give the stage his full attention, I reassure myself that soon, the four of us will be reunited again back at the hotel and when we are, each of us will all have nothing but a fun tale to tell about the enjoyable evening we just experienced.

The first half of the show whizzes by in a blur of beautiful costumes, enchanting songs and top-drawer acting, and by the time the lights go back up again for the interval, everyone in the room is smiling from ear to ear, including my son.

'That was brilliant,' he tells me with a big grin on his face, making it clear just how enamoured he has been throughout the performance so far.

'Wasn't it? Such a good show!' I say, thrilled that Alex's eighteenth year on earth has another memorable chapter to add to it.

Even though both of us already know the gist of the storyline of the production we are halfway through watching, we still spend a few minutes chatting about what we have seen so far, and I'm making the most of this quality time with my son, time that is only going to get more limited as he gets older. Alex has not seen *Phantom* before but has read plenty about it online and studied it in one of his various drama lessons, whilst I have seen another version of it back in England, although this is a much grander stage, so we both have plenty to say. But before we spend the entire interval chatting, Alex tells me he is going to visit the toilet, a need no doubt caused by all the cola he has been slurping since we landed in America yesterday.

As he leaves his seat and makes his way along the aisle to one of the doors at the back that leads out into the main foyer, I take out my phone and see if Jack has sent me anything. He hasn't, but I fire off a quick text to him telling him that I hope he and Maddy are enjoying the game, before confirming that our son is loving his night so far. Then I put my phone away and contently gaze around the auditorium for a few minutes, looking at all the different faces in here belonging to the people who surely enjoyed the first half of the show as much as I did. But while most people are either looking at their phones, their brochures or the person they have come here with, I notice one man standing up on the balcony above the section of the theatre I am in, and he is not looking at any of those things.

He is looking right at me.

I don't think much of it at first, but after looking away for a moment, I glance back again and when I do, I see that the man is still staring at me. It's a little disconcerting, but as I look back in his direction for a third time, I see his eyes are still very much on me, and while I don't recognise him or know why he is looking this way so intently, I get a very bad feeling about it. That's why I turn around and look up the aisle to see if Alex is on his way back to his seat because I feel like I'll be much happier when he is back with me.

But I can't see him, and he still isn't back a few minutes later as the doors at the back of the room are closed, and everyone else retakes their seats for the second half of the show to begin. I glance up to the balcony to see if the man is still up there looking at me, but I can't see him anymore, and a moment later, the lights go out in the room, and we're back in total darkness. But I don't care about what is soon to start happening on the stage because I just want to make sure Alex is okay, and after waiting another minute to see if he comes back, I leave my seat and go in search of him.

It's not easy to make my way down the aisle without any lights to guide me, especially now the actors are back out on stage, and I am blocking a few people's view of the action, leading to several loud tuts and moans from members of the crowd who are probably wondering why I have stayed in my seat all the way through the interval only to get up just as the show is resuming. But I couldn't care less about any of them as I make it to one of the doors and push it open, stepping through into the bright foyer where I see a steward collecting empty champagne glasses over by the bar.

Looking around the foyer, I hope to see Alex, but all I actually see are a couple more employees here carrying out a few of their duties. There is no sign of my son, though I do see the sign for the men's restroom, so I make my way over there.

While I know I can't go in there, I hang around outside the entrance and wait for Alex to come out, but as a few more minutes pass, there is still no sign of him.

Now I'm starting to really worry because knowing how much Alex enjoyed the first half of the show, I know there is no way he would want to be missing the second half unless something very unexpected had happened to him.

Is he ill?

I have no way of knowing without going in there, but I'm the wrong gender to be walking through this door, so I politely ask one of the male stewards if they could possibly go into the restroom and see if my son is okay in there.

The steward is very helpful and tells me he will do that, and after I've given him Alex's name and a brief description of his appearance, the steward goes inside to see if he can locate him.

I wait nervously in the quiet foyer for him and Alex to reappear, and while I can hear the beginnings of a new song starting on the other side of the theatre doors, I don't care that I'm missing out on something fun.

I just want to know that Alex is okay.

'I'm sorry. I checked, but there isn't anybody in there,' the steward says with a shrug when he comes back out of the restroom a moment later, as if the information he has just passed on to me is very inconsequential. But it's not and to prove it, I push past him and enter the restroom myself because I have to see if what he has just said is true.

'Hey! You can't go in there,' the steward calls after me, but I ignore him as I go into the men's toilets and start looking around, opening every cubicle door and calling out to Alex in the hopes of getting a response. But there is none. The only thing I'm getting back is the steward telling me that I can't be in here.

Where the hell is Alex?

I know he's old enough to look after himself now, but that doesn't change the fact that he is not where he said he was going, and after leaving the restroom and rushing back into the theatre, I double-check he is not back at our seats. But his seat is just as empty as mine is.

He's not here.

He's vanished.

Where is my son?

10

JACK

The crack of the baseball as it hits the bat is met with a huge roar as Maddy and I join thousands of other fans in rising up out of our seats to watch the little white ball sailing away into the dark sky, beyond the field and into the stands, meaning a home run has just been scored for the Yankees.

'Wow, did you see that?' Maddy cries, her voice only just audible over the deafening cheers around us, and as music begins pumping from the speakers, the decibel levels only increase in this very noisy section of the Bronx.

'Are you kidding? I knew he was going to do that! He's already hit twelve home runs this season!' I shout back as I clap my hands and watch the player in the iconic navy blue and white pinstriped uniform jogging around the bases and receiving his adulation from the fans.

As everyone retakes their seats, I glance up at the electronic scoreboard and see that it is now 3-0 to the Yankees in the fifth inning, making this a brilliant first half of the game. But it's not just the action on the field that has gone well. I've also been having a great time with my daughter in the stands over the last couple of hours. We've eaten a hot dog, we've had a few drinks, and we've chatted about all sorts of sports-related things as we've sat in our vantage point in the upper deck looking down at the players below. I've also made sure to take lots of photos, too, as has Maddy, and I can't wait to show them all to Lorna when we get back to the hotel. Maybe Alex will be interested in having a look at them as well, and I'll be sure to ask to see the photos he has got from his time at the theatre.

As the music cuts out, the crowd quietens down and the next batter takes his place at home plate. As that happens, I see a rather large man in an extremely oversized Yankees jersey making his way back to his seat carrying two trays of nachos. That's one thing about going to a baseball game in America; it's as much about eating as it is about watching sport, and now that I've seen the nachos, my taste buds are tingling again. That hot dog earlier was good, but with still almost half the game to go, I could make room for more food, and we are on holiday after all.

'How about I go and grab us a few more snacks?' I suggest to Maddy as she films yet another video on her phone.

'That sounds good, thanks,' she replies with a smile.

'Be right back,' I say as I get out of my seat and squeeze my way past a young family who each have a hot dog in their hands.

I jog down a steep set of concrete steps before passing by a burly security guard and making it onto the concourse, where numerous food vendors are located, alongside all sorts of places selling merchandising and memorabilia.

After paying a quick visit to the bathroom and sharing a joke with a very friendly New Yorker, who had clearly had one beer too many this evening, I take my place in the queue for the hot dog stand and start to salivate slightly at the smells of the cooked meat and the fried onions. This is yet another in a long line of unhealthy meals that I've had since I've been stateside, but at least Lorna doesn't have to know too much about this one.

As the queue moves slowly along, I decide to check in with my wife and see how she is getting on across the city, so I take out my phone with the plan to send her a quick message to say that we're having fun and I hope they are too. But when I look at my screen, I am surprised because I see dozens of notifications that weren't there when I last looked at my phone about twenty minutes ago.

They are all missed calls.

And they are all from Lorna.

Unsure why my wife could be so desperately trying to get hold of me, I attempt to call her back, but it's a struggle to get a signal at first now that I'm back inside the bowels of the stadium, surrounded by so much concrete. Realising I need to find somewhere better to make this call, I leave the queue and wander around, checking the signal strength on my phone until it goes back to being high enough for me to contact Lorna. Finally, the phone starts ringing, but it doesn't take long at all for Lorna to answer me.

'Jack! Why haven't you answered your phone? I've been calling you!'

My wife sounds very flustered, and that's why I fear her being angry at me has less to do with me not answering my phone quickly enough and more to do with whatever the reason might be for her calling me so much in the first place.

'Sorry, the signal's not great here, and it's noisy,' I try, but Lorna just launches into her next tirade and when she does, I start to understand why she is so worked up.

'I can't find Alex anywhere!'

'What?'

'I don't know where he is! I can't find him!'

'Wait, calm down. What's happened?'

'He went to the toilet at the interval, but he didn't come back, and when I went to look for him, I couldn't find him anywhere. He's gone! I don't know what's happened to him!'

I'm trying not to panic as much as Lorna is for two reasons. One, I don't know the full story yet, and two, my wife is doing more than enough panicking for the pair of us.

'Have you checked the toilets?' I ask her, but Lorna just snaps back at me to say that it was the first place she checked, and he is definitely not in there.

'Where are you now?' I ask her then.

'Still in the theatre!'

'Okay, could he have got lost? Or be in a different part of the theatre? Maybe he went to a different toilet. He must be there somewhere.'

'He's not here! I've looked everywhere and so have the stewards! This is what I'm trying to tell you; he's gone!'

'He can't have just gone, Lorna. He wouldn't just wander off, would he?'

I'm getting slightly irritated by my wife's hysterics and really wish she would calm down a little and talk this through more sensibly. But that's not happening.

'Of course he wouldn't just wander off! He must have been taken!' she cries, clearly convinced that that is the only possible explanation here.

'What are you talking about - taken? Who would take him?'

'I don't know, but he was enjoying the show, and he wouldn't just leave without telling me, so how else could he have gone unless somebody took him?'

'Just relax. He's eighteen. Even if somebody did try something with him, he's big enough not to go with them.'

'Aren't you listening to me? He's not here, Jack! He's missing!' Lorna cries, sounding utterly terrified, and the more she gets scared, the more I feel the fear too. But as worried as I am about where my son might be, I really can't see how he would have been taken. There has to be a simpler explanation as to where he is.

'He must be there somewhere,' I say, running a hand through my hair as nervous tension begins to take over my body. 'Have you called him?'

'Yes! His phone is turned off!'

'Could it just be on silent? You were watching a show.'

'No, it's off, Jack! What part of that don't you understand?'

'Calm down; I'm trying to help!'

'But you're not helping! You're not here to help me look for him!'

I realise then that I'm going to have to go and get Maddy, and we're going to have to get over to where Lorna is as quickly as possible, whether that is via the subway or a taxi cab.

'Right, text me your address, and we'll come to you,' I say as I head for the gap in the stadium wall that will take me back into the stands. 'In the meantime, is there anyone there who can help you look? Stewards or police?'

'Yes, the stewards are looking, and I'm trying to get them to call the police though they haven't done it yet because they think Alex is here somewhere.'

'Right, well, if they're not panicking yet, then we should try not to,' I say as I walk back out and catch a glimpse of the field below where a Yankees player is jogging to second base and the pitcher for the opposing team is watching him go while shaking his head. But then Lorna says something that causes me to shake my head too.

'What if this is them? What if they've taken Alex because they know we're here and they want to get back at us?' she says with utter terror in her voice.

'Lorna, stop it. This has nothing to do with what happened before,' I say, but my wife is not listening and is now sobbing at the other end of the line.

'This is why I didn't want to come here. This is why I didn't want Maddy or Alex putting anything on social media. I think they know we are here, Jack, and I think they are trying to get revenge on us.'

'Lorna, stop it! That is nonsense, and you know it! Now calm down and keep looking for Alex, and call me when you find him. We'll be on our way, okay?'

I jog up the steps towards my seats and wait for Lorna to reply to confirm that she agrees with that plan. When she does, I hang up and stuff my phone in my pocket before looking for the row on which I was sitting with Maddy. I spot the family of four with the hot dogs who were sitting next to us, so I know I'm in the right place, and then I look past them to where Maddy is.

But her seat is empty.

I look around, figuring I must be mixed up and standing beside the wrong row. But I'm not. This is where we were sitting.

So why isn't Maddy here?

'Hey! Have you seen my daughter? She was sitting right there!' I say, asking the family who were sat beside us.

They all look at me with blank expressions and hot dog meat in their mouths before shaking their heads. But that's not good enough because she was right here when I left her, so they must know where she has gone, and I don't have time for this because I need to get Maddy so we can go and help Lorna look for Alex.

That's why I get angry.

'My daughter! Blonde hair! Blue Yankees cap! She was sitting there! Where did she go?' I cry whilst ignoring the shout from somebody seated in the row behind telling me to sit down because I'm blocking the view.

My loud outburst seems to be the thing to make this family lower their hot dogs and actually help me.

'She went that way,' the father of the family says to me once he's finished chewing his latest mouthful, and he points to the other end of the aisle to where another one of the many entrance/exits in this stadium are.

'She was with someone,' his partner adds then before wiping ketchup off her cheek with a napkin.

'With someone? Who?'

They both shrug.

'Some woman,' the man says.

'What did she look like?'

'She had dark hair. I'm guessing she was about forty. Quite cute,' the man says before receiving a death stare from his partner, who obviously didn't appreciate his comment on the woman's good looks.

I look around for any sign of Maddy or a woman who might match that description, but I can't see anyone. Then I hear my phone ringing, and when I look down, I see that Lorna is calling me again.

'Jack! He's definitely not here! They've gone to check the CCTV cameras!' she tells me as I stand on the steps and stare out gormlessly at the vast, open stadium that surrounds me. All around me are people watching the game, eating food, drinking beer and having the time of their lives.

But I've never felt so alone.

'Jack! Can you hear me?' Lorna cries, and that snaps me out of my temporary trance.

When it does, I let my wife know that this nightmare might be even worse than we first thought.

'I can't find Maddy either,' I confess, feeling a tightening in my chest as I speak. 'Somebody came and took her away while I was out of my seat.'

I don't hear what Lorna says to that because the Yankees hit another home run then, and everybody starts screaming around me.

But I don't make a sound.

I simply watch the ball flying away into the distance, feeling just as helpless as the unfortunate pitcher who threw it.

11

LORNA

This has to be planned. This cannot be a coincidence. Both our children are missing.

So why isn't this police officer taking my concerns seriously?

'Relax, ma'am. We'll find your son,' he says, with an accent as heavy as the sinking feeling in my stomach. 'He might have got lost. It's happened here before. It's a big, old theatre, and there are a lot of doors and corridors. Last month, there was a ten-year-old girl who managed to find herself backstage. One of the sound engineers found her wandering around beside a few of the props. She'd got herself totally lost, but we got her back to her mother, and we'll get your son back to you too.'

'But my son is not ten! He's eighteen, and he wouldn't just wander around!' I cry, the volume of my voice not at all matching the level of respect I probably should be paying this man with the NYPD badge on his shirt and the sizeable firearm in the holster on his waist.

'Ma'am, please. Try and calm down. We'll find your boy,' the New Yorker in his sixties tells me. But while he's probably been in plenty of situations far more dramatic than this one since he began serving this city many decades ago, to me, this is the worst possible thing that could have happened.

It's made even worse now that I know Maddy is missing too.

Jack telling me that he couldn't find our daughter means my worst fears are surely right. This has something to do with what happened here in 2008 just before Jack and I took our kids and moved home. It must be connected. We made a mistake back then and now we are being punished for it, albeit fifteen years later, but still punished all the same.

I thought we'd got away with it, but I should have known better, and I'm angry because I did.

I knew coming back here was not the right thing to do.

I knew we should have never returned to the scene of the crime.

I've been standing with this police officer for the last ten minutes, and I've spent approximately nine minutes and fifty seconds of that telling myself that I need to confess everything to the man in front of me so that he understands the severity of this situation. If I tell him what Jack and I did years ago, then it might help determine how the investigation proceeds now, and I guarantee he wouldn't be telling me to calm down then. He'd see that this can't be a mistake on my son's part and that he hasn't just wandered off like some innocent child. He has to have been taken, just like Maddy surely has. But if I tell him the truth about me and Jack, then the investigation will take a different turn, and it'll start with me and my husband being put in handcuffs, so that's why I've kept our secret to myself for now. But it's about the only thing I am keeping to myself as I launch into another anxious tirade towards this policeman.

'Please, you have to find him! Somebody has him. Just like somebody has my daughter at Yankee Stadium! This has been organised. We've been targeted!'

While the police officer was already aware that my daughter was missing elsewhere, as well as my son, he was probably thinking we are either two very careless parents or we have two very mischievous children. Either that or it's just a huge coincidence. But my using the word 'targeted' seems to be the thing that piques his interest the most.

'Why would you be targeted?' he asks me, lowering the radio he had just been using to communicate with his colleagues and now giving me his full attention.

'Erm,' I say, trying to think of a reason that won't make him want to arrest me. 'I don't know. I'm just saying both our children are missing. Something organised has happened here. Something planned. I just need you to find out what it is.'

'We're looking into everything at the moment,' the police officer tells me, no longer looking at me with quite the intensity of stare he was a moment ago. 'But the simplest explanation is usually the right one, and the chances are both your children have just got themselves a little lost. You're tourists here, right? Lost in New York. It happens, not just in the movies, but in real life.'

The officer goes back to talking on the radio then, and he and his colleague at the other end of the line talk so fast and in such a thick New York accent that I can't understand every word of what they are saying, but when he's done talking, he tells me to come with him.

I follow behind him, matching his swift pace, and as we go, I ask him if he has any news on where my son might be. He says not but they are going to look at something, and I keep close to him as we move through the foyer that will soon be full of people leaving the show that is due to end any minute. While I do that, I check my phone to see if there is any news from Jack at the stadium, but he has not tried to make contact with me yet. I guess he's busy doing the same thing there as I am here, and he'll only update me when he has some news, just like I will do with him.

But which one of us will have news first?

And will it be the good kind or the bad?

I follow the officer into a dusty, old room where I find a skinny guy in the same colour shirt as all the stewards out in the foyer, so I assume he is an employee at this theatre too. He's sitting in front of a very old computer, the ones with the chunky backs rather than the slim, sleek laptops of the modern day. He's looking at numerous grainy images on the computer's screen, and when I realise this is the theatre's CCTV system, I grimace because - based on all the evidence, it seems very old-fashioned. But as the officer leans in and tells the man in front of the computer the exact time we are looking for, I see that he's able to find it quite quickly enough, so that is promising.

I see it because there is my son right there on the screen.

'That's him! That's Alex!' I cry as I point at the screen on which I can see my son walking across the quiet foyer before entering the men's restroom. But now he's gone into the bathroom, we have lost sight of him, which leads to my next question.

'Do you have cameras in there?' I ask, but the answer to that is an obvious one, and the officer beside me looks annoyed that he even has to dignify that with a response.

'What do you think?' he says flatly while keeping his eyes on the screen.

We wait for a very long and anxiety-ridden minute before we see the door to the restroom open, and Alex reappears again. But as he starts crossing the foyer again to return to the auditorium, he is intercepted by a man in a baseball cap.

'Who is that?' the officer asks as we keep watching and as we do, we see Alex having a conversation with this man.

'Is there any sound?' I ask, desperate to hear what they might be talking about but, again, the officer almost finds that question insulting.

My son is still talking to the man until a moment later when they start walking away across the foyer together.

'Where are they going?' I ask, but none of us will know the answer to that until we watch what happens next, and that's when we see the pair of them disappear through a door.

'Where have they gone? Go to the next camera!' I cry, and the man at the computer taps a few keys before the image on the screen changes. Now I can see Alex following the guy in the cap down a set of stairs.

'Why are you following him?' I ask my son out loud even though he obviously can't hear me. But I want the police officer to know that this is very strange behaviour from Alex. He knows better than to just wander off with a complete stranger. He knew that when he was a child, so he certainly knows it now he is an adult.

'Next camera,' the officer says as we lose sight of them again once they've gone through another door, but then we get a grim response.

'There are no cameras there,' we are told.

'What do you mean there are no cameras?' I cry, utterly aghast.

'That's just a side entrance to the theatre. It's not covered by any camera.'

'Why not?'

I'm furious and for good reason because if we can't see where they went, how are we ever going to find them?

The police officer is back on his radio now, and I hear him say the words 'west', which I presume is the side of the building my son was taken out of. I also presume there are police officers on their way to that part of the theatre to see if they can locate Alex outside. But what if they can't? What if he's already gone? What if he's disappeared into the city?

Those are all very frightening questions to consider. But there is one more that I really want an answer to.

What on earth would cause my son to willingly walk out of the theatre with a man he had only just met?

12

JACK

We have about five minutes to find my daughter before the ball game ends and our task becomes infinitely more difficult. That will be when fifty thousand people will leave their seats and pour towards all the exits around this stadium and by the time that happens, we can kiss goodbye to being lucky enough to spot Maddy in the crowd. That is why, amongst many other reasons, I am imploring the policeman and the stadium liaison officer I am with to act quickly. But despite me telling them we have to find Maddy in the next few seconds, they seem to be far less concerned than I am.

'Let's see what we can see on the cameras,' the liaison officer says as we head for the security room and while that sounds promising, the banks of screens I see when we enter the room are overwhelming. There must be over fifty monitors in here, all of them showing various angles of Yankee Stadium, and on each screen are thousands of baseball fans, most of whom look exactly the same as each other because they are all wearing Yankee caps and Yankee jerseys. Trying to spot my daughter in amongst them all is going to be a nightmare, if not impossible, because just like most of these people on camera, she was wearing a Yankees cap too. But we can at least narrow our search down, and after I have shown the officer my ticket, he can tell one of the security personnel in here which section of the stadium we were seated in.

As I take a deep breath and wait for them to find the right camera, I check my phone and when I do, I see that I have lost my phone signal again, meaning Lorna won't be able to contact me if she has any news. At a time like this, it is imperative that the pair of us keep a steady line of communication, but there's not much I can do about that at the moment, and I just have to hope that my wife is having success in her search for Alex in the city while I'm searching for his sister here.

'Okay, what time do you think she would have left her seat?' I am asked, and I have to consult my watch before estimating that it must have been just after nine o'clock.

The footage is taken back to that time, and after zooming in on the row I was sitting at, we start watching. When we do, I see myself on screen and realise I must have been a little early in my estimation of the time when Maddy might have been taken. But a second later, I see myself getting up out of my seat, so I tell everybody else in this room who is watching that this must be when it happened.

As I disappear off screen, innocently on my way to go and get snacks that I would not, ultimately, get a chance to buy, I see Maddy sitting by herself in her seat, her full attention on the game in front of her. As I watch her intently staring at the field, my heart aches because she looks so happy just sitting there being entertained by the baseball players. When I found out I was having a little girl twenty-one years ago, I assumed it would be all pink dresses and shopping sprees rather than baseball caps and sports games, but my daughter turned out to be way more like me than I could ever have imagined.

And now she might be gone.

But then I see her attention taken away from the field because she turns to look at somebody at the end of the aisle. It's a woman in a cap and dark blue jacket, and she is gesturing to Maddy to come with her.

I watch as my daughter gets out of her seat and goes to the end of the aisle before the woman says something to her, and then Maddy quickly follows her down the steps and out of an exit which is one along from the exit I went out of on my way to get the hot dog.

'Who the hell is that?' I cry, stunned my daughter would just leave with a stranger.

'You don't know who that woman is?' the liaison officer asks me.

'No, I do not!'

'She seemed to know Maddy. And Maddy must have known her to go with her.'

'My daughter does not know who that is. We're on holiday here. We're tourists. She doesn't have friends here.'

I've quickly shot down the assumption that Maddy knew the person she went with. But the first assumption is not so easy to debunk.

"She seemed to know Maddy."

Yes, she did.

'Whoever that is, she waited until Maddy was on her own before she made her move,' I say, pointing at the screen and the empty seat where I was once sat happily with my child. 'She appeared as soon as I had gone to get food, so she must have been watching us. This isn't random. It's planned.'

The evidence seems to back my claims up, and along with me telling everybody here that not only is my daughter missing, but my son is too, it's obvious that a very sinister plot seems to be unfolding as we speak.

But how will it end?

As the staff in front of me work to check other cameras and try and find out where Maddy and that woman went next, I step out of the room because I need to get a phone signal back. Thankfully, I find one, and I call Lorna as quickly as I can to update her on the situation.

When she answers, I tell her all about the woman who got Maddy to leave with her, and she, in turn, tells me about Alex leaving the theatre with an unknown male.

'This doesn't make sense. Why would both of them just walk away from us with some stranger without telling us where they were going?' I ask, even though I know my wife is just as clueless as I am on that.

'I'm so mad at them,' Lorna tells me, a little surprisingly. 'Why have they been so stupid? Why would they just go with these people?'

But I get where her frustration is coming from. Even if these nefarious people targeted our children, whoever they are, their plot would surely have failed if Maddy and Alex had just done what they would have been expected to do and not gone anywhere until they had spoken to their parents.

Unless they were threatened.

Coerced.

Left with no other choice.

'I don't know what to do,' I confess to Lorna, never having felt as helpless as this in my life before, and that's including what happened fifteen years ago, because at least then I was in control of certain things and could make a plan that kept my children safe. But now Maddy and Alex are missing, I'm reeling and lost, and the more time that passes, the less in control of this situation I start to feel.

'I do,' Lorna says just as I hear a roar go up around the stadium, and I guess that means the game has just finished and the Yankees have won.

'No, Lorna. Don't you dare. That will make things worse, can't you see that?'

'I don't care, Jack. Our children are missing, and it's all our fault. We don't know where they are or what's being done to them, but this isn't their fault; it's ours. They don't deserve this.'

'Lorna, please! Just wait for a second!'

Hundreds of people are now pouring onto the concourse and within seconds, it is thousands, and now I'm completely surrounded by delighted baseball fans who have just had a very enjoyable evening at the ballpark.

As they all chat and cheer, I put one finger in my ear while pressing my phone tightly to the other one so that I stand a chance of hearing what Lorna is saying at the other end of the line.

'If we tell them the truth, then they might be able to find them faster,' Lorna says. 'I'll tell the police here and you tell them there, and maybe they can get Maddy and Alex back quicker.'

'No, Lorna, do not say a word to the police about what happened! I mean it. If you do, we are finished!'

'Jack, it's our children!'

'And this is our family!' I cry, my voice loud, but nobody around even looks at me because of the overall noise in this packed concourse. 'We stick together, and at the moment, with Maddy and Alex missing, each other is all we have. We need to be able to talk and to figure this out, but we won't be able to do that if we're arrested and put in separate prison cells, will we?'

I don't hear what Lorna says next because some drunken fan sings loudly as he passes me, so I carry on with what I was going to say next anyway.

'We need to be together, not on the phone like this. I'll come to you, or you come to me - whichever, I don't care. We just need to be with each other, and then we'll talk properly, okay?'

Again, I don't hear what Lorna's response is, and when I look at my phone, I see her end the call, sending a shiver down my spine.

Did she hear me? Did my message get through to her? Does she know that she is to hold off on doing anything until we are together again? Or is she confessing everything to a police officer at this very moment and, in the process, ensuring this family is destroyed even if Maddy and Alex turn up safe and well soon?

I see the door to the security room open and a police officer look at me and as he does, I wonder if he wants me to come back in there with him to ask me more questions about Maddy or if he has just been told over the radio to arrest me for a very serious crime that has gone unsolved in this city for fifteen years.

All the while, as I stare helplessly at him and wait to see what happens next, the fans around me keep acting as if winning a game of baseball is the only thing that matters in the world.

13

MADDY

The blindfold that covers my eyes ensures that I can't see where we are going, but I know we are in a car because I can hear the engine and feel the movements as we turn the corners. I can also hear the voices of the other people in this car with me, though they haven't said much so far. Just a few simple things like 'I hate the Bronx' or 'Take a left here.'

One of the voices belongs to the woman who spoke to me at the stadium and the one I have to blame for me being in this scary situation now. The other voice is male, and while I have no idea who he is, I'm guessing he's the one who put his hand over my mouth and bundled me into this car before the blindfold went on and I was told to comply or I would be killed.

I'm unable to remove my blindfold because my hands are tied behind my back, and there is a seatbelt across me that is keeping me from sitting too far forward, so overall, I feel totally trapped. My phone has also been taken from me and I know that because I felt a hand go into my jeans pocket shortly after we started driving.

'Where are you taking me?' I ask for the second time since this journey began, but just like the first time I enquired, I get told to be quiet. If it wasn't for the fact that I'd heard the man mention he had a gun a few minutes ago, then I would keep asking again and again.

More than that, I'd be screaming and hoping to attract the attention of anybody outside this car who might hear me and be able to help me. But because my life is under threat, I go back to being quiet, and as the car moves on, I think about how we must be getting further and further from the stadium and, at the same time, further and further away from Dad.

He must know I'm missing by now, and I expect he's very afraid, as well as very confused. Not only will he be wondering what has happened to me, but he'll want to know why I just left when we were having such a good time together. It was more than a good time; it was a great time. I was having such fun with Dad at the game, and if only he hadn't got up to go and get us some snacks, maybe I'd still be there now watching the game finish and cheering with the rest of the crowd. But he left his seat, and that was when things started going wrong.

Dad had been gone for a few minutes when I heard somebody calling my name, and when I looked to the end of the row, I saw a woman gesturing for me to come closer. I had no idea why she wanted to speak to me but the fact she knew my name, as well as how much urgency she had, told me I had to know what was going on, so I left my seat and went to talk to her. When I reached her, she told me that my father had suffered a fall on the concourse and while he was going to be okay, she had come to get me so I could see him in the medical room.

It's only now that I know it was just a fictitious story designed to get me to follow the woman, but how was I to know that at the time? As far as I knew, Dad was hurt and wasn't able to come back to his seat, so of course I was going to want to go and see him and make sure he was okay. That was why I followed the woman out of the stands and through the concourse and down a staircase and, ultimately, all the way to one of the exits at the stadium. All the while, I was asking questions about Dad, trying to determine the extent of his injuries and what might have caused him to fall over. I was so sad about the thought of him sitting in some medical room with a sore head or bloody knee that I was just desperate to get to him because while I was worried about him, I knew he'd be worried about me too and would want to put my mind at ease by telling me he was fine.

The woman didn't say too much as she led me away, just that he would be okay and that they may be able to get us tickets to another game because this one had clearly not gone to plan. I remember thinking how nice that gesture was, even though we were only here for a few days and wouldn't be able to come back again, and maybe that's why it took me a little longer than it should have to realise that something was wrong.

We just kept walking and walking, and it was only when we got outside that I started to get suspicious. That was when I was suddenly bundled into a parked car and within seconds, the doors were locked, and we were on the move. By then, it was far too late for me to get away, and I knew I'd been tricked.

Instead of me going to see Dad, I'd just been taken from him.

But why?

I tried to get my captors to tell me why they were doing this to me, but I've not had a proper answer yet, so my imagination is running wild with theories. I've accused them of making a mistake and getting the wrong person because surely, they didn't mean to kidnap me, right? I told them I was just here on holiday and that I'm from England where nothing like this ever happens. I've also told them that if they want money, then they only have to ask my dad for it because he will surely give it to them.

I've told them he works for a bank, though I'm guessing they might already know that if they targeted me, and if they need cash, he will happily give it up to ensure my escape. But no matter what I've said, this nightmare hasn't come to an end yet and the longer it goes on, the more I'm fearing this is going to end badly for me.

Are my friends back home going to see me on the news over there?

British woman kidnapped in New York.

What will they think? I'll be famous but for a really bad reason. I don't want to be famous. I don't want people talking about me or looking for me.

I just want to go back to Dad.

I wonder if he has spoken to the police yet or if he is still looking for me on his own, running around the stadium and feeling scared and upset because he can't find me in the crowd. Hopefully, he knows that I would never just wander off on my own, and that means he might already have the police out there looking for me. There must be cameras that saw me get pushed into the back of this car, and I'm hoping we're going to be followed very soon by lots of cops with flashing lights on the roofs of their cars and guns to match the one my kidnappers have.

But I can't hear any sirens. All I can hear is the engine and the sound of the tyres on the road beneath this car, and we are still getting further and further away.

'Please, just let me go,' I beg, no longer interested in questions or answers. 'I just want to go home.'

'Shut up,' comes the heartless response, and as tears soak into my blindfold, I bow my head and wonder how my life could have ended up like this. I was so happy to be in New York, and I was happy at university back home. I'm not even twenty-one yet and have got so much to look forward to. But now, it might all be taken away from me.

Suddenly, the car comes to a stop, and I start panicking because I fear it means the end for me. But then I hear the car doors open, and I'm pulled outside. Then I'm told to walk.

'Where are we going?' I ask as I'm marched somewhere I can't see, but I get no answer, and all I can hear is the sound of the gravel we are walking over. Then the noise ceases and I feel warmer, suggesting I have gone indoors again. But where am I?

'Staircase,' I'm told before I'm led down a set of steps, but it's hard when I can't see, and I almost lose my balance a couple of times, only kept upright by the man holding tightly onto my arm. Then I hear a door opening ahead of me before I'm pushed forward, and a moment later, my blindfold is pulled off.

Her Husband's Mistake

When it is, the first thing I see is shocking.
It's my brother.
Whoever these people are, t*hey have Alex too.*

14

ALEX

While it was shocking to see my sister pushed into the same room I'd just been put in, it did at least give me some comfort to realise that I wasn't alone in this. But it's a small comfort because now I know I'm not the only one who is in danger here.

'Are you okay?' I ask my sister once the man who just brought her in here has left the room and locked the door behind himself.

'Alex! What's going on?' Maddy asks me, and she looks as terrified as I feel.

'I don't know,' I tell her, and while I'd love to give her a hug, it's impossible with my hands tied behind my back. Hers are tied too, meaning all we can really do is stand opposite each other and look around at this place we now find ourselves in.

We're in what appears to be some kind of a basement, or maybe it's a small room in an old, abandoned building or warehouse. I have no idea because all I can see are bare brick walls, and there is a strong, musty smell in here. There are no windows to help us either, and while we have enough space to stand up straight and walk around a little, there's absolutely nothing else in here we can do. There's no food or drink or any way to call for help. Just the two of us locked in this place somewhere in New York, far away from where our parents are probably looking for us.

'What happened to you?' I ask Maddy, eager to know how she came to be in this room because while I have my own crazy story, she must have hers too. I'm right because she tells me all about the woman at the baseball game who told her that Dad had suffered a fall, and she had followed her believing she was being taken to see him. After that, she was blindfolded and driven away from the stadium until she got here. Then she asks me how I got here.

'I went to the bathroom during the interval at the theatre,' I begin, thinking back on how such a simple decision led my captors to have the chance to take me. 'When I came back out, there was a man there waiting to speak to me. He asked me if I did any acting and when I said yes, he said he was a casting director who kept an eye out at shows like this for any talent.'

I'm already shaking my head as I tell the story because I can't believe that I fell for such a stupid lie. I was so gullible and got far too excited at hearing the words 'casting director' that I lost all of my common sense. Everyone always says if it sounds too good to be true, then it probably is, but I completely forgot that as I listened to the man ask me if I could spare two minutes to go and meet a colleague of his who was responsible for putting together the cast for an upcoming production in the city.

I did think about asking if I could run back into the auditorium and tell Mum where I was going but then I was afraid I might miss my chance, and the last thing I wanted to do was be the actor who missed his big break because he was too worried about telling his mummy where he was. I knew that sometimes, actors got the role that changed their life not because they did well at an audition, but because of a chance encounter in a random place and maybe, after so many failed auditions through my teenage years, it was going to be a chance encounter that got me into the acting world. Who knew, it could be the story I was one day telling on a late night chat show on TV after the host had asked me how I got started.

I figured we'd be quick and once I got back to Mum, even if she was a little annoyed that I'd been gone a while, she'd have not only understood, once I'd told her what happened, but she would have been delighted for me too.

That's why I didn't bother going to her and just went with the man instead.

With my head filled with dreams about how I was just about to be plucked from obscurity in England and given a juicy role in a star-filled New York production, I followed the man through a side door, and we left the foyer behind. As we went down a set of stairs, I was already visualising the conversations I would have with my friends back home. How I would tell them that dreams come true and that they would have to fly out to be at the opening night of the show that I was going to be starring in. I was even thinking about James and how even though I would miss him terribly, maybe one day, when I was rich and famous, he might realise he felt the same way about me as I did about him.

With so much on my mind, I guess that was why I didn't realise something was wrong until it was far too late. By that point, I'd been pushed into a car, handcuffed and blindfolded and then driven away too, the end of my sorry story matching the end of my sister's.

Now, here we are together, both guilty of being gullible and falling for a lie.

But just how bad is our situation?

'Why is somebody doing this to us?' Maddy asks as we move away from the door and stand closer to the back wall opposite it, both of us eager to put a little more distance between us and the next person to potentially come in here. Unless those people are going to be Mum and Dad? I didn't expect my sister to join me here, so maybe our parents will be here next.

'I don't know,' I reply, watching the door, but so far, it's not opening again.

'What do you think they want? Money?'

'Maybe.'

'Do you think they've hurt Mum and Dad?'

'What? No.'

Maddy looks upset and like she is about to cry, so I tell her everything is going to be okay, even though I don't know if that is true. It's different to when we were younger and she would look after me in her role as the older sibling, but at the moment, I seem to be handling this situation slightly better than she is.

But only just. The truth is I am as scared as her, if not more, and while I'm not on the verge of tears, I am trying my best not to panic. But my head is filled with all sorts of questions.

Questions like:

What if nobody finds us?

What if this door doesn't open again?
What if we're just left in here to die?

'Did they say anything to you when you were in the car?' Maddy asks me whilst just about managing to keep her tears at bay for the time being.

'Not really. They just kept telling me to be quiet or they'd hurt me,' I reply. 'You?'

'Same.'

It's then that I start to feel slightly less afraid and a little angrier because I hate the idea of my sister being pushed around and threatened. I'd rather they just kept me here and let her go, but it doesn't look like that is going to happen. But now we are together, and maybe we can work as a team to get out of here.

'If they come back in here, then we need to just rush at them and try and overwhelm them,' I say, hoping my plan doesn't sound as shaky as my state of mind is at the moment. 'If we could surprise them, then maybe we could get away. Or if not, I could at least distract them, so you might be able to run for it.'

'No, it's too dangerous. And even if it worked, I'm not leaving here without you.'

'We just need one of us to get out and get help,' I say. 'If one of us can tell Mum and Dad where we are, then they could find us.'

'No, we stick together,' Maddy tells me. 'We make sure the other one is safe.'

I nod my head when I realise she is serious about not wanting to get out of here if it means I am left behind, and now we are committed to sticking together whatever happens, we think about what exactly might happen next.

'Whatever it is they want, I hope Mum and Dad can give it to them,' I say, nervous because it might not be the case.

'Me too,' Maddy replies.

Then the two of us sit down with our backs against the cold wall, and with little else to do in here but worry, we stare at the door and wonder what the reason it eventually opens again might be.

It might open again because we're being allowed to leave.

Or it might open again because someone is coming inside to kill us.

15

LORNA

I spent another hour at the theatre before it was decided that I should accompany an officer to a police station where I would link up with Jack, and we would assess what had happened tonight from there. By that point, the show had finished, and the theatre was empty, barring everyone but me, a couple of police officers and the theatre's employees, who quietly swept up in the auditorium and looked a little sheepish whenever they saw me standing in the foyer looking bereft.

I'm not sure if they were feeling guilty that a theatregoer could have lost their son here or whether they were thinking this was a big overreaction because my son was eighteen and was probably big enough to look after himself. Either way, they didn't say anything to me except the one kind lady who asked if she could get me some water.

I was initially reluctant at the idea of leaving the theatre, with it being the last place I'd seen Alex, and wondered if it was the best place to stay in case he appeared again. But as time went by, it seemed less likely Alex would show up, and with Maddy missing too, it was considered best if both parents got together at the station, where we could be spoken to by a person with a little more authority than the officers who had been helping us so far.

That person was a detective.

The first thing I noticed when I entered the inner-city police station after being driven here from the theatre is the energy inside this building. If I thought it was busy outside, then in here is almost just as chaotic. Everywhere I look there are men and women in bulletproof vests and firearms on their person, striding through doors with great purpose and while some of them disappear out the door and into the night, almost just as many are coming in to take their place.

I have one experience of being in a police station back in England, but that was a very different experience to this. That time when I entered the station, it was almost more like I was turning up for an appointment with my doctor or dentist, and after speaking with the person sitting behind the desk, I took a seat in a waiting area until someone was ready to see me. But this place does not quite have the same vibe, and as I hear lots of boisterous shouting and watch as four swaggering officers stride past me and leave the building, I guess it's just another reminder of how far from home I am now.

Even though I lived in New York before, one thing that I never got accustomed to was the crime rate here. The news was always full of reports of the more alarming stories, and while Jack always told me not to pay too much attention to it all, it was impossible to take his advice, particularly when I was trying to raise two little ones in the city. It wasn't just the vests and the guns and screeching sirens that filled me with anxiety, but how there were different words for certain crimes in America, and those words always seemed scarier somehow.

Serious crime is called a felony. Burglary is grand larceny. And murder becomes homicide.

I don't know why but to me, those words always seemed more frightening.

Now I'm standing in one of the many hubs of the NYPD, but unlike all those times in the past when I heard about crimes in this city that affected people other than me, this time, I'm right in the middle of it all.

But at least I'm no longer alone.

'Hey,' Jack says when he enters the big and busy waiting room and sees me, rushing over and trying to take me in a hug. But I pull away from him before he can embrace me, and even though this is surely not the time or the place, I tell him exactly why I am not ready to accept his welcome.

'This is your fault,' I say, pointing a finger at his chest. 'This is happening because of what you did.'

'Lorna, calm down,' Jack says whilst looking nervously around at all the other people in here to see if any of them have just heard me. Between all the mobile police officers and the stationary civilians sitting in chairs, there are plenty of folks around who could easily eavesdrop on our conversation and then pass on what they just heard to somebody who might be very interested in learning more about what I mean. But if Jack thinks that is my biggest concern at this moment in time, then he is sadly mistaken.

'You know it's the truth,' I say, my voice still louder than my husband would like it to be. 'We're here because a detective is going to speak to us, and when they're ready, I'm going to start at the beginning with them.'

'The beginning? Lorna, wait. We'll be arrested.'

'Don't you see? Maybe that's what the kidnappers want.'

'Kidnappers? We don't know for sure that they are kidnappers.'

'What world are you living in? Maddy and Alex have been taken, and we've got the CCTV evidence to prove it!'

'No, all we know is that they were led away but not by force. They willingly went with these people, so I'm not sure that qualifies as kidnapping.'

'Are you insane? They were obviously tricked and once they fell for it, they were taken. If they weren't, then we wouldn't be here right now, would we? All four of us would be back at the hotel!'

'Lorna, just try and-'

'Mr and Mrs Thompson?'

We are both interrupted then by the sound of a female voice to our right, and when we look, we see an African American woman in a blue suit and white blouse standing beside us.

Despite having plenty to say to Jack a second ago, I've suddenly lost my voice, so it's my husband who answers for the both of us.

'Yes,' he says.

'I'm Detective Davis. Come with me.'

Jack and I share a nervous glance before we follow the confident woman who is already striding away from us and as we follow her through a couple of sets of double doors, I feel Jack take hold of my hand and when he does, he leans in towards me.

'Please, just stay quiet until we hear what she has to say,' he urges me, but I don't make him any assurances as we reach the room we are to be spoken to in, and Detective Davis invites us to take a seat.

The sound of the chair legs scraping across the hard, uncovered floor in here is loud but not quite as loud as the door closing when the detective shuts it. Then things go very quiet as she takes a seat opposite us and puts her hands on the table.

'I have some news on your daughter, Maddy,' Davis says, and as the words leave her mouth, I feel utterly helpless to stop what might be the worst thing I'm ever about to hear. Is she dead? Or have they found her alive and well?

'A camera near Yankee Stadium picked her up in the back of a car leaving the scene around the time she was reported to have been taken,' Davis says.

'A car?' Jack asks. 'Whose car?'

'We don't know yet, but we're assuming the plates have been changed, and while we're doing our best to try and track its route across the city, it's difficult.'

'Why was she in a car?' I ask.

'Again, we don't know, but we will find out,' Davis says, her words matching the confidence her posture already carries. When she says that, I see Jack's own posture stiffen beside me.

'What we need to know at this moment in time is whether or not the two of you can think of any reason why your children may have been targeted,' Davis asks. 'Because it's clear both of them were specifically approached and led away from each of you, and finding them is going to come down to figuring out why that might have happened.'

I guess this is the perfect point for me to jump in and tell the detective what she is hoping to hear, which is that I do have a very specific reason why I think Maddy and Alex were approached and led away from us. But clearly sensing that, Jack speaks before I can.

'I think this may have something to do with us having lived here before,' he says, and I turn to him, surprised because I wonder if he is going to be the one who tells the truth here rather than me.

'When did you live here?' Davis asks, seemingly interested in this information.

'Between 2002 and 2008,' Jack goes on. 'I was working here.'

'Okay, and why do you think that is related to what's happened tonight?'

'I don't know; I just assume it is. Maybe these people who have taken our children knew us back then.'

'Why would anybody do that?'

Jack goes quiet again then, leaving Davis to ask the obvious question.

'Did you make any enemies in that time?'

'Enemies,' Jack repeats before scratching his head. 'I'm not sure about that.'

'I am,' I cut in, and while the detective's eyes widen with interest, Jack becomes increasingly flustered beside me.

'Lorna,' he says, his voice dripping with the warning he has already given me many times before. But I know that all I need to do is just ignore him and say what I have to say and if I do, the detective might have a lead to pursue to help us find Maddy and Alex.

So why can't I say it?

Detective Davis stares at me and waits for me to finish what I was clearly about to say, but when I fail to speak again, she prompts me.

'Mrs Thompson, do you and your husband have any enemies in New York?'

'Erm,' I begin, before Jack quickly intercepts.

'Detective, what I'd like to know is what you and your team are doing right now to find our children because you know this city better than us, and it's your job to help us. The last thing you want is for this to become an international news story because it's hardly the best advertisement for your city if tourists aren't safe here, is it?'

My husband has quickly put the heavy lifting in this conversation back onto the woman who is supposed to be here to help us and, at the same time, steering it away from the very delicate subject we were dancing perilously close to. Not only that, but he has rather cleverly hinted at this becoming a very bad case of PR for New York and its police department, something that I'm sure he's not bothered about himself but the person he is speaking to might be. But the detective is not stupid and knows we were close to just potentially revealing something important, so she doesn't allow herself to be swayed so easily.

'I can assure you that we are looking into why both your children seemed to go missing on the same night, but we require cooperation from all parties, including you,' Davis says. 'If there is anything you are hiding, then not only will I eventually find out what it is, but the delay in doing so may make all the difference between this matter having a positive outcome.'

There is a knock at the door then and Davis gets up to answer it, giving Jack the chance to let out a very deep breath, but just before the detective opens the door, I pick up on something she just said.

'What do you mean our children *seemed* to go missing on the same night?' I ask her, very curious at that choice of words.

Davis stops and looks back at me before answering.

'We have to look at all possibilities, and while you think they may have been taken, it could be that they willingly left and are perfectly safe and well. If so, no crime has actually occurred here.'

'No crime?' I say, shocked that the detective could even be thinking such a thing, but she opens the door then and shares a few whispers with the man outside the room before she excuses herself and steps out fully, closing the door behind her.

With Jack and I alone together again, we have the chance to carry on the debate we were having just before the detective introduced herself to us. But neither of us does that. That's because we're wondering how this could possibly be anything other than a crime.

But what if it is somehow innocent? Could it be that simple? Could the kids be safe and if so, could this have nothing to do with what happened before?

We still don't know.

This is a rare situation in life where our children know far more than their parents do.

But just how much do they know?

16

MADDY

I don't know how long my brother and I have been in this room for because we have no way of telling the time, nor can we see outside to get any idea of whether it's still dark or if the sun has started to come up yet. All we do know is that we are both very tired, though it's impossible to rest because neither of us wants to lower our guard just in case things take a turn for the worst.

'This is our fault,' Alex says quietly after a moment.

'How so?'

'We were the ones who wanted to come here. It was our idea to come to New York.'

'Yeah, because we wanted to see some cool things, not get kidnapped by a bunch of psychos.'

'Maybe this is why Mum and Dad moved back home with us. It's dangerous here.'

'I know plenty of people who have come to New York before, and none of them have ended up in a room like this.'

I tell Alex to stop being so stupid, and we go back to sitting in silence for a moment. But then we hear footsteps on the other side of the door, and when a key turns in a lock, we both quickly get to our feet, trying to be prepared for whoever might be about to come in here.

But when we see who it is, both of us are immediately disarmed because it's not quite who we were expecting. Rather than some big man with a weapon, it's a woman who, I would guess, is in her early fifties and not only does she look very unimposing, she looks a little apologetic to have disturbed us.

'Hello. How are you two doing in here?' she asks, which is a very strange question to begin with.

'Who are you?' I ask as Alex and I keep our backs to the wall behind us, aware that appearances could be deceiving, and this woman might be far more dangerous than she looks. But if she is, she is doing a very good job of appearing quite placid because she steps aside then and allows a man to enter the room behind her. When he does, I see he is carrying a chair and he places it down in the middle of the room before stepping back out again. Then the woman gives us another smile before taking a seat.

'My name is Nancy,' she says as she looks from my brother to me and back again. 'Hello, Madeline and Alexander. It's nice to meet you.'

It's disconcerting not only for her to say our names, but use our full ones. Neither of us have had those used since we were young, mostly because, to us, they don't sound quite as cool as the abbreviated versions we like to go by now. But this woman is being polite, which, in these strange circumstances, just makes me even more nervous.

'How do you know who we are?' Alex asks her as I study the woman's calm demeanour. She is wearing a stylish jacket and dark trousers along with a pair of shoes that I know are expensive because I've seen them on a reality TV show before. She also has a thin gold watch around her left wrist, and I get a better look at it when she lifts her hand to tuck back a strand of her dark hair behind her ear.

'I know who you are because I know who your parents are,' comes the simple response, and that is the first strong clue that this has more to do with them than us.

'Our parents? What about them?' I ask, eager for more information.

'What do you know about them?' Nancy asks us, which sounds like another very unusual thing to say.

'I know they're going to kill you if you don't let us go,' I snap back, feeling quite pleased with myself for about a second at how fiery I have just been. But if I was hoping to make this woman think twice about what she is doing, then I guess it hasn't worked because she doesn't look flustered at all.

'You think they're capable of killing a person?' Nancy asks.

'Yes,' I say, doubling down on my threat to her because I want her to be afraid and fear what she has done. That way, she might let us go before this gets any worse. But what she says next leaves Alex and me stunned.

'I guess you know them even better than I thought then.'

'What do you mean?' my brother asks her.

'The thing is,' Nancy says, crossing her legs and letting her hands rest on her lap. 'Your parents are not quite who you think they are. They did something very bad in this city and until today, they have escaped

120

punishment for that. But now that they have come back, things are changing.'

'What did they do?' I ask as I notice Nancy looking sombre.

'They took something from me,' she says quietly. 'Something I cared about more than anything else in the world. But even worse than that, they didn't own up to it. They lied and got away with it and because of that, they caused even more damage.'

This all sounds crazy, and I'm struggling to see how she could be talking about my parents here. Mum and Dad, the two people who brought me and Alex up? Plain old Lorna and Jack who are always telling me what to do and who spend most of their evenings sat at home on their sofa in front of the TV?

They've done something wrong?

'Look, I don't know what you think you're doing here, but there's obviously been a mistake,' I say. 'Just let us go, and we won't say anything to anybody. We just want to go back to our hotel and get some sleep, and we're going home soon. We'll probably go home on the next flight once we get back to Mum and Dad. Whatever happens, you don't have to get in trouble for this if you just let us leave. Isn't that right, Alex?'

I look at my brother to make sure he is in agreement with me because I need him to help convince this woman that she can avoid prison if she does the right thing now. But while he doesn't say anything to disagree with my plan, he doesn't do what I want him to.

'What did Mum and Dad do?' he asks.

'I just told you,' Nancy replies. 'They took something very dear to me, and after they lied, they took something else too. There's a reason I am sitting in this room alone rather than beside my husband.'

I frown then because the mention of her husband has me confused. Who is he, and what has he got to do with this? That is what I'm thinking. But the longer Nancy is here, still looking very calm, the more I'm wary of asking her questions because the things she comes back with are very troubling.

'My husband is not here because he took his own life,' Nancy goes on, and Alex and I share a nervous glance. 'Yes, if you're wondering, he did so because of what your parents did.'

'Our parents haven't done anything wrong,' I try again, but Nancy just shakes her head dismissively.

'Sadly, that's what you and everyone else thinks. But I know the truth, as do Lorna and Jack.'

'Then why have you waited so long to do something about it?' Alex asks, making a good point. 'Why wait all this time if they did something years ago?'

'That's easier said than done,' Nancy tells us. 'Thankfully, you won't know what it is like to suffer the grief I have but if you did, you would understand that it's hard enough just to get out of bed in the morning at a time like that, let alone plan revenge. But my husband did try.'

'What do you mean he tried?' I ask.

'I'm right in saying there was a fire at your family home in England seven years ago,' Nancy says, and Alex and I both gasp because it's true, though we don't know how this woman knows it. 'You all survived, and it was believed to have been an accident, but it was not. My husband started that fire when he knew you were all inside, and his intention was to burn you all alive. I knew nothing of it at the time. I didn't even know he'd left the country. If I had known his intentions, then I would have told him just to kill your parents, not you innocent children. But a man intent on revenge is a powerful thing, and I doubt I would have been able to dissuade him even if I had known about it beforehand.'

'Your husband started that fire?' I ask in disbelief, my memory recalling that terrible night when I was thirteen years old and ran from my house with flames all around me. I can still remember the heat on my skin and the fear in my heart as I worried not only for myself, but for the rest of the family. I didn't see how all four of us could make it out alive but we somehow did, mainly thanks to Dad and his bravery in refusing to leave any of us behind.

Now this woman is saying her husband started the fire that almost killed us all?

'Yes, that was Bob's work,' she says, using her partner's name for the first time. 'I only found out when he came home and told me where he had been and what he had done. As far as I knew, he'd been at a business meeting in Florida, but he soon set me straight. I was shocked but not angry. But he was. He was furious. That's because he knew you'd all survived. Every single one of you. I feared what he might do next after that. I figured if he was willing to fly all the way to England to try and get his revenge, there would be no stopping him then. But I was wrong. Even though that day wasn't technically the day my husband passed away, I will always count that as the real day he died because that was when I saw the light go out in his eyes, and he became just like me. Helpless. Depressed. Ultimately, he did not see the point in going on because he felt your parents would never pay the price for what they did.'

Nancy puts a hand to her face then and wipes away a couple of tears while Alex and I stand and watch her in stunned silence. After a moment, she is ready to go on again.

'My husband took his own life,' she says, her eyes vacant as she utters the words. 'After that, I figured things couldn't get any worse and mostly accepted that I had to let it all go. The only way for me to keep living was to forget about your parents and move on, and somehow, that's what I'd managed to do, for the most part anyway. But I always kept tabs on you as a family in England, and when you two started using social media, I kept tabs on those accounts too.'

'You've been watching us on social media?' I ask, well aware that all my accounts are public, meaning it's not just my followers who can see what I post, but anybody who types in my name.

'How else do you think I knew you were coming to New York?' Nancy asks me, and for the first time since she came in here, she displays not a kindly smile or a despondent gaze, but a satisfied smirk, as if she is showing there is a fiery streak beneath the calm veneer.

It's hard to think that my brother and I posting some innocent photos and updates online has potentially led to us being in this room now, but it seems that way. That is when I suddenly realise why Mum was so adamant about me not posting anything about New York online. Did she know it was a risk to be here?

'When I saw you were coming back, all of you together as a family, I knew I had been mistaken,' Nancy says. 'I realised then that I couldn't let it go, not really. Not ever. So, I made a plan. I had you followed when you landed here, and when I saw my chance, I had you both taken. Now, for the first time in a very long time, I have something I should have had a long time ago. I have your parents' attention. That's because I possess their most precious things in the world. And do you know what? It feels good.'

Nancy stands then, the smirk still on her face, and as she heads for the door, Alex and I have numerous questions for her. But she ignores all of them, and as she walks out, I know she only came in here to let us know the truth.

We're not in here because of her.

We're in here because of Mum and Dad.

17

LORNA

It's a little disconcerting to see that the sun has risen over New York as I make my way out of the police station to begin my journey back to the hotel. As far as I knew, it was still dark outside, but that's mainly because there were no windows in the police station. But now I've seen that a new day has dawned, it only makes my situation seem worse. Maddy and Alex have been missing for a whole night now, and with a new day beginning, I'm left wondering how many sunsets and sunrises I will have to go through before I see them again, if ever.

'Thank you,' Jack says as the police officer who will be driving us back to our hotel opens the door for us to allow us into his vehicle.

I follow Jack into the back of the car, and once the door is shut and the driver is in position, we begin our route back to the hotel. It's that time of the morning when it's early enough for the buzz of the city to have begun but not quite late enough for the roads to be snarled up with traffic, and I'm grateful for that because I want this journey to be quick. The longer I'm cooped up in this car, the more I'm going to be trapped with my thoughts, and that cannot be a good thing.

'Everything will be okay,' Jack says to me as he takes my hand and gives it a squeeze, but I don't even look at him as he speaks. I just keep my eyes on the window and on the people we are passing on the sidewalk. I'm so envious of them all because they are unburdened by the woes I have. Their hearts haven't been ripped out by losing their children in a vast city, and they aren't waiting to be alone so they can start crying. They're just on their way to work, probably thinking about that TV show they watched last night or which restaurant to try and make a reservation at this weekend. Such simple things, and things I used to be occupied with too. But now my concerns run far deeper, and as the car travels on, I find myself hating these people for how easy their lives are compared to mine.

Without really thinking about what I'm doing, I remove my hand from Jack's grip, separating myself physically from him, which is hardly a supportive thing for a wife to do, but it's just what I felt like doing. He says my name in an attempt to get me to look at him then, but I ignore that too and keep my head turned away from him, my eyes on the streets outside and not on the man who is suffering just as much as I am.

Jack rather sensibly doesn't try to talk or touch me again until we have got to where we are going, no doubt aware that to do so may result in a dangerous argument that the police officer in the front could hear. We sit in silence until we reach our hotel, and as Jack thanks the driver, I just stare at the bellhop at the entrance doors and feel like crying right here. The bellhop himself looks puzzled at the appearance of the police car outside this expensive property, and whilst normally he would be rushing to open the doors of any vehicle that had parked outside here, he is understandably hesitant to do so this time. I guess it's not every day a police car comes to the hotel, and he can hardly be expecting anybody on the back seat to be a paying guest here. That's why Jack and I are left to open our own car doors, not that it's a huge problem because we're used to having to do things for ourselves. But as we walk towards the door, the bellhop still seems unsure about our presence here until Jack shows him our room card, and he suddenly breaks into a big smile and welcomes us back.

The lobby is quiet when we go inside - not too many guests are up and about at this early hour - and I'm glad we are not going to have to share the elevator with anybody on the way up. The last thing I need is some other tourist making small talk with us in between floors, wishing me a good morning and saying that 'New York sure is a fun place, isn't it?'

Jack and I leave the elevator in the same manner we left the police car and that is in total silence. We stay that way as we walk along the carpeted corridor to our hotel room door but just before we go in, I pause and stare at the door beside it. It's the door belonging to the room Maddy and Alex share, and I'm thinking about how they should be in there now, still asleep, exhausted from a fun day yesterday and getting the final rest before another day of fun today. But they aren't in there, or at least I assume they aren't. But suddenly, I'm desperate for a possible chance at escaping hell, and I wonder if this horrible situation might end up having a very simple solution.

What if Maddy and Alex are in their room? What if they did somehow end up coming back here and despite all my worrying, they are actually safe and well in their beds? Could it be that easy?

'We need to get a room key for their room,' I tell Jack, and even though he doesn't share my level of optimism that it will lead to anything, he sees I am serious so has no choice but to follow me back downstairs to the lobby where I ask the man on the desk for a room key. It takes some explaining on our part as to who we are and why we need the key, but once the employee has seen that it is our name on the booking for both rooms, as well as having heard the exceptional circumstances which we're in, he gives us the key we require.

I rush back up to our floor, and while Jack continues to tell me that it's unlikely they will be in their room and that I shouldn't get my hopes up, I'm still praying this will all be over in a moment.

Tapping the room card on the door, I hear the electronic click to tell me that it has unlocked before I push the door open and burst in, calling out to Maddy and Alex and telling them to get up because whatever prank they have just pulled is over and they should apologise to their parents now. I also make sure to say out loud that I am not even going to be mad at them because I just want them to be okay, but all Jack does is keep saying my name as he scurries behind me and tries to get me to slow down.

Then I see them. The two empty beds. Both unslept in. No signs that either one of my children have laid their heads on their pillow overnight. As if that's not quite enough, I rush into the bathroom to check in there, as if I'm going to find one of them in the shower and the other in front of the mirror brushing their teeth. But that room is empty too, barring the toiletries that both my children have, where they left them, of course.

It's stupid, but the sight of both their toothbrushes by the sink is the thing that sets me off crying and even though Jack tries to hug me, I push past him and escape the bathroom only to be back in the bedroom looking at their suitcases and the clothes they were saving to wear for later in the holiday.

The tears are uncontrollable now, and as I let out a very loud and very primal cry of pain, I feel Jack's arms envelop me, and he squeezes me tightly, preventing me from rushing around this hotel room anymore while at the same time, shushing me and trying to soothe my cries of pain.

I completely give in to him then, allowing him to hold my body weight as I sink down and let all my emotions flood out of me. Now we're both on the floor and while I'm still crying, he just looks ashen. We stay right there on the floor for ten minutes until we are interrupted by a knock on the door and when Jack goes to answer it, I hear somebody ask him if everything is alright. I also hear the words 'reports of a loud noise coming from this room' and 'I'm required to check if everything is okay in here.' The next thing I know, Jack has opened the door a little wider to allow the hotel employee to see inside and when he does, he spots me curled up on the floor sobbing. That will take a little explaining, but I leave that job to Jack, and as he talks to the concerned employee and explains to him exactly why I am in such a mess on the carpet, I close my eyes and give in to my exhaustion.

But it's not just the exhaustion of a sleepless night and extreme anxiety about the wellbeing of my two children.

It's the exhaustion of mentally carrying the memory of what Jack and I did fifteen years ago, a secret I feel I am finally ready to share with someone else now and will do just as soon as I can get myself up off this floor and away from my husband long enough to do so.

It's time I told my story.

The police need to hear what they should have heard a long time ago.

18

LORNA

2008

'Have a good day, darling,' I say to Maddy just before she goes racing away across the playground to join her friends. I smile as I watch my little girl go because not only is her enthusiasm contagious, but it's just a joy to see her so happy here. Every parent worries about whether or not their children will make friends at school and even more so when living abroad, and I've spent a lot of the last five years worrying if my daughter might struggle to fit in with the American kids with both her parents being English. But I'm pleased to say that Maddy has settled in well at elementary school, and as I watch her chatting away with two girls I recognise as her friends, Phoebe and Clara, I keep smiling before I go and say a quick hello to both those girls' parents.

After a little gossiping at the gate, I finally walk away from the school, and now it's just me and Alex, my cute little boy who is keeping a tight grip on my hand as we walk back home. Unlike Maddy was at Alex's age, he is very quiet and gets noticeably more tense whenever we drop his sister off at school, which tells me he is wary of big crowds and so many other children. But he still has a few more years to go until he starts at this school and by then, I expect he might be a little more confident about things, as well as have a few friends that he will have made from kindergarten and various play dates I help arrange for him with other mothers.

As the two of us walk back along the street, we are passed by numerous fast-moving cars, most of which are driven by parents who, having just dropped off their little ones at school, are now racing to get to their workplace in the city on time. But I have no such concern because all I have on my agenda for the rest of the day is to spend quality time with my son, and I'm grateful for that as we pause on the edge of the sidewalk before spotting a gap in the oncoming traffic and carefully crossing the street.

We make it back home ten minutes later, and my mood is good, helped somewhat by it being a crisp, clear day in NYC. I love it when the sky is blue because it just makes this city feel so much cleaner, and after months of rainwater and snow on the pavements through a brutally cold winter, it's nice to be able to go outside and not get wet feet. I'm also pleased because I had been planning on going into the city today with Alex, although such a trip was always going to be weather dependent, but now that it's a sunny day, there is nothing that might cause me to delay.

After getting home and giving Alex a snack, I gather up everything I'll need today and put it into my handbag before we're ready to leave the house again. But just before we go, I send Jack a quick message to tell him what my plans are, as well as wish him a good day himself. I know he won't reply because he'll still be driving, but he'll see my message when he gets to where he is going, and it'll make him smile when he does.

He's at a work conference in Greenwich today, which I believe is a suburb in Connecticut, our neighbouring state, and the place he is going is about fifty minutes or so outside the centre of New York. He wasn't thrilled about having to make a long drive or sit for eight hours in a stuffy room all day and listen to boring banking experts drone on about fiscal matters, though it does mean he didn't have to take the crowded subway into the centre of the city at rush hour like he usually would have to do. Instead, he gets a nice drive out to a less condensed area, and it will do him good to get away from the crowds, for a short while at least. As I also told him, it will do him good to hear what the so-called experts in his field have to say about the current state of the economy because there are some worrying things being said on the news at the moment, and it would help if we could get a little reassurance about it all.

Not wanting to dwell on potential money worries until I really have to, I put my attention back on my little boy, and after we leave home, we make the short walk to the subway where we board a train bound for W 34 St/Broadway station, which is the closest stop to where we are going, and it's a place that I just know Alex is going to love.

We're going to the biggest toy store in New York.

Oozing with excitement because my son has no idea just what a treat he is in for today, we sit together on the swaying subway as we move beneath the depths of the city, and while I chat to Alex on occasion, I stay quiet for the most part because I know he likes to just watch all the other people in the carriage. He's only three, but he's already an accomplished people-watcher, and after staring at and studying a fellow passenger for a moment, he will often ask me who they are and where they are going. At first, I would tell him they were probably just a local going to work, but then I realised he liked it when I made up fantastical stories about these strangers so I do that now instead. It's much more interesting for him to hear that the old man on the subway is a dragon fighter on his way to buy a fire-proof coat of armour before his next big battle rather than admit he is probably a municipal worker just counting down his days to retirement.

But it's not just my son doing a little people-watching because I can't help but do the same and as I do, I notice many people on the subway are reading newspapers with fairly grim headlines on the front pages. There are more warnings of a financial disaster to come, but I just tell myself that it is journalists scaremongering and expect that Jack will come home tonight with much better news for me that is based on fact rather than fiction.

We get off at our stop shortly after, but Alex still has no idea what is waiting for him once we make it back to street level and as far as he knows, we are just going to the park. But I see his face light up when he spots the toy store and everything in the window of it up ahead, and after I take him inside, I know he's going to be happy enough to stay here for as long as I'll let him.

In total, we spend over an hour in the toy store, and I'm pretty worn out by the time we leave, as well as a hundred dollars or so lighter in my bank account. But Alex had a great time exploring the huge store, and that's all that matters. We head to the park then, where we spend the rest of the morning, and it's just after I have started thinking about what we might do for lunch that I take my phone from my handbag to check the time. It's the first time I've looked at it since I messaged Jack earlier, but he hasn't replied to me. I guess he's very busy at his conference, and I almost feel a little guilty for spending my morning in a toy shop, although as a full-time mum, I'm busy enough.

Deciding that I'd rather take Alex home for lunch than spend a fortune on something in a café in the city, we board the subway again and head for our house, and by the time we reach our destination, all Alex cares about is getting inside so he can finally play with some of the toys I bought him earlier. But I get a shock just before we walk through the door because I see Jack's car parked outside, which is very odd because he told me the conference did not finish until 5 pm.

So why is he home at midday?

I'm wondering if he might have decided to come home for lunch, but that seems unlikely given how long it would have taken him to drive here and then go back again, so I'm starting to think that the conference might have been cancelled and he's been given the rest of the day off. But again, that would be unlikely because with how limited his annual leave is here, I doubt Jack's employers are just handing out days off like confetti. Maybe my husband is sick, which is worrying, so I rush inside to check on him. When I do, I find him sitting at the kitchen table nursing a bottle of beer.

'What are you doing?' I ask him, and my first thought when I see the sorry look on his face is that it was bad news at the conference, and the looming financial crisis is far worse than we thought.

Has he lost his job already?

In hindsight, I would really wish unemployment had been the extent of our problems.

Jack goes to answer me but then sees Alex and that seems to be what stops him. Then he just stares at our son with a very weird look on his face, and while Alex is thrilled to see his daddy is home, I know this is not normal.

'Alex, go and play with your new toys in the playroom, and we'll be with you in a minute,' I say to my son, quickly leading him away from his pale father, and once Alex is occupied with his toys outside of the kitchen, I go back to see Jack, who is still sitting at the table.

'Jack, what's going on?' I ask, bracing myself for some bad news.

'Something bad has happened,' is all he says before taking a slug of beer.

'What?'

'I've killed someone.'

I stare at him and wait for him to say something else because that doesn't make any sense. But he doesn't speak. He doesn't say another word.

'Is this a joke?' I ask him, wondering if he and his friends have come up with a stupid game to play on their partners.

'No,' Jack replies, and I know he means it when I see tears in his eyes.

'What have you done?' I ask as I stay where I am, too afraid to get any nearer for the time being.

'I was driving to the conference, but I was running late. I couldn't find the damn place, and my satnav wasn't being much help,' Jack says, running a hand over his beleaguered face. 'And I was distracted by what they were saying on the radio. All this talk about the economy collapsing. It's got me so stressed out.'

Jack drinks again to prove just how stressed he is, but all I can think is how all of what he has said just sounds like bad excuses for something terrible he has done.

'Jack, what do you mean you killed someone? How?'

'I wasn't paying attention to the road. I was looking at the satnav and listening to the radio and trying to find the damn conference and worrying about losing my job and how we would afford the mortgage on this place, and then-'

Jack ends his sentence abruptly, but I force him to go on.

'I hit a kid,' he tells me, and when I see the fear in his face as he looks at me, I know it is true.

'You hit a kid? With your car? What kid? Where? Are they ok?'

'No, they're not ok,' Jack says as he stares at his beer bottle. 'He's dead.'

19

JACK

PRESENT DAY

I've been standing in the shower for a while just allowing the hot water to run over me, but I'd have to stay in here for a lifetime for it to have any chance of washing away the sins of my past. As always when I'm alone, I'm tormented by what happened that day fifteen years ago and as always, thinking about it and regretting it does not make it better. Now, my kids are missing, and regardless of whether or not their disappearance is linked to what I did in 2008, I know that either way, I deserve to be in this hell.

Call it karma or whatever.

All I know is that I deserve to suffer.

As this bathroom steams up, I think about Conrad, the thirteen-year-old boy who I struck with my car and then left by the roadside after I'd got out to check on him and found him without a pulse. I know his name because it was on the news that night after another driver had done what I should have done and reported the body lying in the road. All that time I'd been praying for some other news story to dominate the headlines beyond the constant reporting of the dire economic situation but when it happened, it was not the story I needed.

Son of millionaire businessman dead in hit and run.

While the term 'hit and run' is frightening enough, the news also used another term common in Connecticut where the accident took place, and that was 'Evading Responsibility'. That was exactly what I had done, and well aware of how guilty I would be found if I was brought to justice, I had gone online not long after the incident to see what the possible maximum jail term would be for causing death and leaving the scene.

20 years.

That awful number had been running round and round in my head as I had made my way home from the scene of the crime after I had decided to forgo the conference and return to safer ground. I knew the house would be empty when I got back because Lorna had told me she was taking Alex into the city, and it was, which had been of some relief because it gave me a little time to process it all in peace. But the silence had become unnerving, and it was almost even more of a relief when Lorna got back because then I had somebody to share my burden with. But needless to say, my wife was stunned by my admission.

As I remain beneath the hot water, I grit my teeth and feel like punching this tiled wall beside me because I would give anything to be able to go back in time and change so many things about that day. While it would be obvious to say that I would have been paying more attention to the road so that I would have seen Conrad when he stepped off the pavement, that's not the only thing I wish was different. Going further back than that moment my car hit him, I would change the fact that I'd stayed up extremely late the night before drinking downstairs and worrying about the prospect of losing my job in the impending recession while Lorna slept in our bed, completely unaware that I was awake. If I had only tried to get some sleep instead of sitting up worrying, then I would have been in a better state of mind to focus on the road that next morning. I also wouldn't have potentially been over the drink-drive limit from all the beers I consumed while sitting by myself through the dark hours of the night. I didn't stop drinking until just before sunrise, so I must have been over the limit.

Being sleep-deprived, a little drunk, worried about my job and struggling to use a satnav to get to my destination are just all bad excuses for what I did. But there is no excuse for what I did afterwards. I didn't have to run. I could have stayed with that teenager and held him until the paramedics arrived, even if it wouldn't have made much of a difference to his chances of survival. I could also have waited for the police officers to arrive on the scene, so I could have given them a detailed account of exactly what had happened, meaning both they and the victim's family had a clear understanding of it all. Sure, that would have most likely resulted in me being taken into custody and facing serious charges, but maybe if I was honest and expressed my remorse, I might have escaped with less serious punishment.

Who am I kidding?

I knew my life would have been ruined if I had stayed, so I did the cowardly thing and ran.

And I've been running ever since.

After I told Lorna my shameful secret, she had quite rightly told me that I had to talk to the police before I left it any longer, and when I said no, she volunteered to be the one who did the talking for me. But I didn't let her call the police and tell them what I'd done because I shamelessly told her how it wouldn't just be my life that was ruined if the truth came out.

Hers would be too, as would the kids.

If I went to prison, then not only would I lose my job and the work visa that came with it, Lorna would be left alone to raise two kids by herself, and she'd have to do so back in England, far away from where I was serving out my sentence. Not only would she be missing my support, but she'd be missing my income too, as well as being stuck in the tough position of having to explain to our children and our family and friends what I had done. Not only would it have been the end of our adventure in America, but it would also have been the end of us as a family, and I implored Lorna not to throw away everything we had together over me making one awful mistake.

Perhaps it would have been better if she had ignored me and told me that I had brought all of it on myself and that it wasn't her fault our lives were ruined, but mine. Maybe it would have been better if she had made that call to the police and then got on a plane back to England with the kids. Who knows? I could have served my sentence in an American jail and paid my penance and been back home to rebuild my life guilt-free, or at least be far less burdened now, having owned up to what I did.

But I guess I'll never know because Lorna, ultimately, did as I begged her to.

She didn't report me to the police. She stayed quiet and gave me a chance to get away with it.

And get away with it I did.

The water is starting to scald my skin, but I don't turn off the faucet and give myself any relief because I don't deserve it, nor do I deserve my wife's support or the two wonderful children I raised.

I don't deserve it after robbing two parents of the wonderful child they had.

Bob and Nancy Williamson. Those are the names of Conrad's parents, and they are the poor souls who not only had to identify their son's body, but go on national television and appeal for information about who might have killed him.

As the media was quick to report, this was no ordinary crime against an ordinary family. The Williamsons were famous in Connecticut for being one of the wealthiest families in the state, and they proved it when they offered a $1 million reward to anybody who gave them information that could result in the guilty party's arrest. But nobody came forward in those early days after the incident, and I guess that was because nobody saw me, meaning Lorna and I were the only two people in the world who knew what had happened. But after both deciding to keep quiet about it, we were not keen to tempt fate and stick around to see if we got caught, so I made the decision to quit my job and take us all back to England.

I told my employer that I was worried about the upcoming recession while Lorna packed the bags and took Maddy out of school, and before long, we were almost ready to go. I'd already sold my car as quickly as I could, but selling the house would take much longer, and while the latter stages of that could be completed with us overseas, the beginnings of it required us to be in New York so that we could find a realtor and get the paperwork in order. That delay in things meant we were still in America when Conrad's funeral took place, not that I planned on being anywhere near it.

But my wife had other ideas.

I could scarcely believe what I was hearing when Lorna told me that she had gone to the cemetery where Conrad was being laid to rest and watched from a distance as his loved ones had paid their respects. I told her it had been incredibly risky of her to go there, but she assured me that she had kept her distance and nobody had seen her and that she had only done it because her guilty conscience needed her to complete some form of a kind act to make it feel slightly better about the whole thing. But while I still thought she had been mad for going there, it was too late to change it, just like it was too late to change everything I had set in motion in terms of us moving back to the UK, and precisely two weeks after the incident, I boarded a plane at JFK Airport with my family.

We flew back to England, intent on never returning again.

From what felt like a safer distance, I followed the news online and read all about Bob and Nancy Williamson and how their marriage fell apart after the loss of their son. They divorced, seemingly unable to stay together once they were bonded not by love but by a shared grief so horrible that the only way to get over it was to create a distance between them. But while I felt incredibly guilty about that, I felt even worse when I saw a news story years later in which it was reported that Bob Williamson had died in an apparent suicide. He had taken one of his small sailing boats out into the ocean and allowed himself to slip into the water, leaving behind on deck only a short letter to his ex-wife beside a photo of their beloved late son.

I turn off the shower just as I finish running through the whole sorry story in my mind, and as I stand and allow the water to drip off my body before I speed up the drying-off process with a towel, I contemplate whether my wife could be right. Could this be the Williamson family, or what is left of it, somehow taking their revenge on us? Did Nancy figure out it was me who killed Conrad and after waiting for us to return to America, has seized her chance to make me suffer? But it can't be. How would she know I was behind the wheel of the car that day?

This has to be about something else. But what?

Where the hell are Maddy and Alex?

And am I going to ever find out, or will I be left in limbo like Bob Williamson was just before he couldn't bear it anymore and took his life?

I quickly dry myself with one of the soft and fluffy hotel towels before unlocking the bathroom door and stepping out, allowing plenty of the trapped steam to escape into the cooler room beyond. I'm expecting to find Lorna lying on the bed where I left her napping just before I went to take my very long shower, and while I plan to let her rest, I will get changed before heading back to the police station to seek an update on my kids.

But then I see the bed is empty.

Lorna is not here.

She can't have gone far, so I get dressed as quickly as I can before running out of the room and rushing to the elevator before taking it down to the lobby. I'm hoping to find my wife down there, perhaps talking to somebody at the reception desk or possibly standing outside beside the bellhop, getting a little fresh air. But I don't find her in the lobby or at the hotel entrance and after trying and failing to reach her on her mobile phone, I find myself looking at all the people on the sidewalk and wondering how I've ended up losing my wife as well as my children.

More than that, I'm wondering why Lorna has left without saying a word.

But the more I think about it, the more it makes sense.

She's gone to tell the police the truth.

And she didn't want me to stop her.

20

LORNA

I had to get out of that hotel room. I'm not exactly proud of the way I did it by pretending to be asleep and waiting until Jack was busy in the bathroom before I snuck out but at least I got out of there, and now that I'm alone, I have some space to think. It's still early, but the city has fully come to life, and all around me are people busily beginning their day.

This is the New York I know.

The New York I used to love.

The smell of coffee and bagels in the air. The roar of machinery from various construction sites as new skyscrapers are built or older ones are renovated. And the hustle from all those who aren't just going to work today because it's their duty but because it's their only way to survive in this expensive place.

I've always been both mesmerised and intimidated by this city's energy in equal measure and never more so than today as I wander aimlessly through the crowded streets whilst doing two things. One, I'm hoping I might get lucky and catch a glimpse of Maddy or Alex out here amongst the sea of faces.

Two, I'm looking for a police officer to go and confess all my sins to.

Being the wife of a killer does not come with a rulebook. There are no instructions or guides. It generally comes down to whether you do the right thing or the wrong thing.

Report your partner to the police.

Or protect them.

So far, I have chosen to protect Jack, and that is why nobody knows he killed Conrad Williamson on a bright, sunny day in 2008. But it wasn't just out of the sense of duty I felt as a wife that I didn't get my husband in trouble with the police. It was because I was being selfish. I liked my life, or at least I did just before Jack told me what he'd done. I loved being his wife, and I loved being a mother, and together with our little kids, as a unit of four, we were brilliant. I didn't want to do anything that would break that unit up, and that was why, ultimately, I decided not to go to the police.

Jack will still think to this day that the reason for me keeping quiet was because he was able to persuade me to do so. But it's not all about him, as much as he might think it is. It's about me and my mistakes too. Him not looking at the road properly that fateful morning was not the only mistake that day. I made a mistake when I stood there in the kitchen of our old house and realised that I couldn't watch my husband get taken away in handcuffs and be left having to look after two children on my own.

Jack has been selfish for not wanting to go to prison.

And I have been selfish for not wanting to be left on the outside without him.

My heart skips a beat when I see what I think is a police car coming to a stop at a red light ahead of me, but then I relax a little when I see that I am mistaken. If it had been so, then I would have had no choice but to go over and tap on the window, and then, after attracting the driver's attention, I would have told him everything. But it's not to be, at least not quite yet, as I watch the car drive away before I turn a corner and enter a new block.

I might like to think that I'm walking aimlessly, but I'm operating on old memories, and that's how I know that if I keep going in this direction, I will soon end up in Times Square, and there are always lots of police officers there. I'll have no trouble finding somebody to listen to me then. But as if reading my mind, after so many years living with me, my phone is ringing in my pocket and when I take it out, I see it is Jack calling me.

I don't answer the phone, and after two more failed attempts at speaking to me, he sends me a couple of text messages. The first one makes it seem like he is just concerned for my wellbeing.

Where are you? Are you okay?

But the one that follows shortly after that shows he is more concerned about his own.

Please don't do anything stupid. We need each other.

I put my phone back into my pocket without replying to Jack, and as I walk on, I think about how much he must be freaking out back at the hotel as he panics about what my next move might be. But what is about to happen has been long overdue, and while I'm sure he can't see it yet, he will understand one day that telling the truth was the best thing we could have done.

He's terrified about being incarcerated, but I believe the truth will ultimately set him and me free. But if it's already too late for our consciences to be eased, at least we might be able to do something even more valuable than that, and that is potentially get our children back.

When I think about what I would do if my child had been killed in a hit and run and nobody had been brought to punishment for it, it breaks my heart because I can't imagine living in that pit of fear and despair over not getting justice for my little one. But when I think about what I would be willing to do if I suspected somebody of that crime and felt I had to take justice into my own hands, then it scares me even more because I know there is very little I wouldn't do to make that person pay.

That's what is happening here. Nancy Williamson must have somehow figured out that Jack and I know what happened to Conrad and because of that, she has chosen revenge.

I don't know how she knows.

Or maybe I do.

Maybe it has something to do with me going to her son's funeral.

Jack was stunned when I told him that I'd attended that grim event, but I felt it was the least I could do, a sort of sordid way of me paying my respects to a youngster who had his whole future robbed thanks to the man I married. I kept my distance from the burial party and thought I hadn't been seen, but I guess I was. How else would Nancy have known to look at me and us? And how else would she have set up the poaching of our children less than twenty-four hours after we had landed in New York on our first trip back to this city since it all happened?

As I catch a glimpse of a couple of the giant screens that make up just a fraction of what is on show in Times Square, I know this will all be over very soon and when it is, the only thing that matters is Maddy and Alex are safe. Nancy will be holding them somewhere now, and she will only let them go if we do the right thing. There have been no threats or ultimatums from her, though. She's obviously decided just to leave this up to Jack and me to figure out, but that's her prerogative. No need to get the police involved on her part. She probably doesn't even trust them anyway, not with how they have done so little for her in the past. She's taken matters into her own hands, and who can blame her? Maybe I'd have done the same in her position.

But would she do the same as me in my position?

Would she willingly confess to a crime that will ruin her family?

As I arrive at Times Square, I see plenty of things I expect. Tourists. Commuters. Police officers. It's the latter group of people who I make my way over to, and as I approach the group of four NYPD officers standing outside the giant retail store that has a huge photo of a famous basketball player hanging in the window, I'm ready to be the mother my children need me to be.

Then I hear my phone ring again.

Assuming it's Jack, I almost leave it, but some weird sixth sense makes me check anyway, as if there is a chance it could be Maddy or Alex telling me they are actually okay after all, and I don't need to confess to the police officers standing right in front of me. A couple of them have noticed me approaching them and turn to listen to what I have to say, probably assuming I'm just a lost tourist about to ask them for directions rather than a tormented woman about to tell them that her husband killed a young boy and now I want my children back from his mum.

But when I look at my phone, I see it is an unknown number calling me and as I answer, I take a deep breath because I have a feeling I might know who this could be.

It turns out that I am right.

'Hello, Lorna. Nancy Williamson here.'

21

LORNA

'Are you okay, ma'am?'

The question from the NYPD cop is a friendly one, but I don't answer him. I just stay standing frozen in front of him with my phone pressed to my ear and the whole of New York swirling around me.

'Ma'am?'

'Walk away from the police officer,' Nancy tells me through the phone, so I do as she wishes, smiling politely at the cop to let him know that I am fine before leaving him behind and scurrying away down the sidewalk.

'Well done, Lorna,' Nancy says as I look in every direction to try and spot her because it's obvious that she is watching me, and she must be in Times Square with me somewhere. But I can't see her, not that I have much chance with so many other people in this part of the city, though I guess Nancy prefers it that way anyway.

'Were you just about to do what I think you were about to do?' Nancy asks me, and there is almost a devilish lilt to her voice, as if she is taking some pleasure in knowing just how difficult such a thing would have been for me.

'Do you have my children?' I ask her, firing a question back at her, though I have no idea if she will answer it because she may wish to keep leading this conversation. But she does.

'Yes,' she replies calmly.

Wow. There it is. Confirmation that the nightmare is as bad as I feared.

'Are they okay?'

There's a brief pause this time, and I start to panic.

'Nancy!'

'Your children are safe,' she tells me. 'For now, at least.'

I feel a huge weight lift off my chest and shoulders because while I don't have Maddy and Alex back yet, at least I know they are still alive. That tells me I'm not too late to save them, and the fact Nancy has called me must mean she is going to give me a chance to do so as well.

'What do you want?' I demand to know.

'Aren't you going to ask me why I have your children? Isn't the answer to that question troubling you so?'

I don't say anything to that and that allows Nancy to scoff.

'No, of course you don't need to ask me because you know why, don't you? You know exactly what you and your husband did, and you know exactly why I have done this to you both now.'

'How?'

'How do I know you killed my son?'

Again, I choose to say nothing to that.

'Besides the fact that you haven't said anything to make me think otherwise since this phone call began, I have known it was you ever since I had you followed after Conrad's funeral.'

There it is. The confirmation that I made a huge mistake in going to the funeral that day because, as Jack feared after the fact, I had been seen, and I had made myself into a suspect by being there. But just because I was present, it doesn't necessarily have to mean I was guilty.

'How do you not know I was just in the area or had seen the story in the news and had stopped to pay my respects?' I try.

'Well, that may have been so, but I thought it prudent to look into you all the same, just in case, and I'm glad I did because what I found out was very telling.'

I keep walking slowly through the heaving square as Nancy speaks, occasionally having to put one finger in my other ear whenever a loud New Yorker starts shouting nearby or a taxi blares its horn as it drives past. But other than that, I can hear her clearly enough, which is not necessarily a good thing for me.

'After I had you followed and looked into, I learnt that you and your husband seemed to be cutting all ties with the city and attempting to move back to England as quickly as possible. The house went up for sale, the car was sold, and if I didn't know any better, I'd say you were running from something.'

Nancy has us all figured out, but I don't go ahead and confirm it for her quite yet.

'But, of course, it could have all just been a coincidence that you were at the funeral and that you were moving back to England shortly after. I didn't have any proof, but I thought I might as well see if my suspicions led anywhere, so I did some more digging and was interested to learn that your husband had been due to attend a conference in Greenwich on the day Conrad died. In fact, the venue the conference was being held at was only five minutes away from the location where Conrad was hit.'

Another car horn. Another loud shout. My finger goes back into my ear again.

'What was even more interesting was that I learnt your husband had not actually attended that conference after all. I wonder what could have happened for him to unexpectedly not be able to make it? Traffic problems perhaps? Car trouble? A diary clash? Or maybe it was because he had struck and killed an innocent teenager and fled the scene before anybody could catch him.'

'Nancy, listen-'

'No, you listen to me, you cold, callous bitch. I know what your husband did, and I know that you knew about it at the time too. Did you really think you could get away with it? You took my son!'

Nancy's change of tone from calm and collected to furious is extremely unsettling, almost as unsettling as trying to have a conversation like this in the middle of one of the busiest places on Earth.

'I'm sorry,' I say, not even denying it because there's no point in doing that, not if I want to see my children again. 'I'm so, so sorry.'

'I bet you are now that I have Maddy and Alex,' Nancy snarls back. 'But you weren't so sorry before that, were you?'

'I don't understand. If you were convinced it was Jack, why didn't you go to the police?' I ask her. 'Nobody ever came and spoke to us. You could have had them question us before we even left.'

'Don't you think I tried that?' Nacy replies quickly. 'I spoke to the police and gave them your names, and I thought they would question you. But they didn't. They were too busy looking into other leads and theories, things that, ultimately, didn't amount to anything, and by that time, you'd already gone. The police were even less interested in looking into you once they found out you were in England.'

'I don't get it. Why didn't they try and help you?'

'There wasn't a lot of sympathy for me and my family at that time,' Nancy tells me. 'We'd recently donated quite a large sum of money to a politician who had got into power and made several large budget cuts in the NYPD. Once that was common knowledge, I had a feeling the police weren't going to be as eager to solve the case as they could have been. I've made up for it since by donating more to the NYPD, but the fact is, they weren't as willing to help us back then.'

I shake my head at what I'm hearing, but it doesn't change my predicament, nor does it alter Nancy's train of thought.

'I kept tabs on you, and you seemed happy enough back in England. I figured you'd never chance coming back here again. But I was wrong. You did. Once I knew you were in New York, I wasn't going to miss my chance.'

'You've been watching me all this time?' I ask.

'You best believe I've had eyes on you ever since you landed at JFK,' Nancy tells me. 'Before that, when you were in England, I couldn't do much, at least not until your children were old enough to start using social media and documenting their lives online. I've never had you watched in England, though my late husband did.'

The mention of Bob Williamson, Conrad's father and the man who tragically took his own life after failing to deal with the loss of his son, shuts me up as Nancy goes on, seemingly hitting her stride now.

'Bob did much more than keep tabs. He actually went to England, and he went to your house.'

'What?'

I'm stunned because I had no idea he had been anywhere near us.

'That's right. He stood right outside your front door. He looked into your windows.'

I feel cold as I hear all of this. But I feel even worse when I hear why Bob didn't make his presence known to us.

'And he stood and watched your house burn down to the ground.'

My mind instantly flashes back to the night I was woken up by our smoke alarm, and after jumping out of bed and running out of my bedroom, I looked down the stairs to see flames consuming the hallway below.

'Bob started the fire?'

'Yes, he did,' Nancy confirms. 'He wanted to see you all burn.'

'My children were in that house!' I cry as I startle a passer-by who unluckily happened to walk past me at that moment.

'Yes, and his child was already dead. He didn't care about you or your family. Not after what you had done to ours.'

I can't believe what I'm hearing, and as my mind takes me back to that awful night when I thought all four of us were going to die, I can't fathom how Bob could have just stood out on the street with a grin on his face watching it all happen.

'Alas, he didn't get what he wanted that night. Nobody died, meaning he was still left in a world of pain while you got to continue enjoying your family. There was a big change in my ex-husband when he got back to New York after that. He was much quieter and seemed far less consumed with the idea of revenge. All he did then was drink, right up to the day he took his boat out and never came back.'

I'm not sure what Nancy expects me to say to that, but if she is hoping I will be sympathetic, then she is severely mistaken because any sympathy I had for that man has now evaporated after learning he was the one who started that fire.

'I'm glad he's dead,' I say, and while it comes across as incredibly harsh, I mean it because that man almost killed my children.

'I thought you might say that,' Nancy replies, unaffected by my outburst. 'And you're right. He is dead, and I have to deal with that on top of losing a child.'

I'm just about to say I'm sorry for the fact she has lost so much through no fault of her own when she speaks again.

'But now it is time for you to join me,' Nancy says.

'What do you mean?'

'You have a choice, Lorna, just like you had a choice about whether or not to confess to what Jack had done.'

'I was just about to go to the police!' I cry.

'I know you were, but I stopped you, and let me tell you why,' Nancy goes on as New York grows ever busier around me. 'You can become a widow, or you can lose your children; it's up to you.'

'What the hell are you talking about?'

'Lorna, you have options here,' Nancy says, and normally, a person being given options would be considered a good thing. But then I hear what my options are, and unfortunately for me, they could not be any worse.

'Either you kill your husband for me or I kill your children for you.'

22

LORNA

I try to comprehend the ultimatum that Nancy has just given me, while I look all around Times Square to see if I can get any idea who she has here keeping an eye on me. Her watchers could be any one of these people in this crowded hub, or maybe she is here herself, and I just can't spot her amongst the crowd. Or perhaps she is up in one of the many tall buildings that overlook this famous part of the city, looking down at me and smirking with her phone pressed to her ear. I don't know because I can't see her or anyone else who has eyes on me. But I know they are out there, just like they've been out there ever since I got here, and that's why I know they will continue to watch me, whatever I decide to do next.

But what will I do?

'What?' I say, pretending not to have just heard what Nancy said, though it's obvious by my very long pause that I did and that I've just been too shocked to respond.

'You heard me,' Nancy says. 'Either you kill Jack or I will kill Maddy and Alex.'

'That's crazy! You can't do this!' I cry.

'Who are you to tell a person what they should do? You are a criminal, Lorna. You have been harbouring a fugitive for the last fifteen years and not only that, but you had the gall to return to the scene of the crime for a damn holiday as if you were rubbing my face in it along with the memory of my ex-husband and son! You are in no position to tell me what I can or cannot do, so quit wasting time and make your choice!'

'Nancy, I can't. The police can have Jack. I'll tell them everything, and he'll be arrested. I will be too, I guess. But just let my children go. They don't know anything about what their parents did, and they don't deserve this!'

'You think I'm just going to give you and Jack the chance to get a good lawyer and weasel your way out of this?'

'We wouldn't do that. We'd confess!'

'Yeah, right. Maybe at first but once your kids were safe, then you'd just say you were coerced into confessing, and you'd try and get out of it.'

'No, we wouldn't!'

'You expect me to believe that? You've already avoided justice once!'

'It's different this time! I just want Maddy and Alex back, then you can do whatever you want to us.'

'Then what I want is for you to kill your husband,' Nancy says cooly. 'I want that man dead for what he did to my son. For leaving him by the curb like a piece of roadkill. I don't want him to go to prison and one day get out to resume his life because that wouldn't be enough. I want him dead! I want his future stolen, just like he stole Conrad's!'

Nancy has made herself perfectly clear but even so, what she wants is not exactly easy. In fact, it's downright impossible. I can't kill Jack and even if I did, I'd never get away with it.

'Nancy, please. This isn't right. Let the police arrest Jack, and let justice be done. I know it's far too late, but he is willing to pay for what he did, and so am I. Nobody else needs to die.'

'You mean nobody who you care about needs to die?'

'No, I mean-'

'I know exactly what you mean. But I know exactly what I want, and this is the only way you get Maddy and Alex back. I want Jack dead by the end of the day. Either you kill him or he kills himself, though I suspect he is far too cowardly to make it easy for you. But if he is dead and I have confirmation of his body by midnight, then Maddy and Alex will be released back to you and this will be over, once and for all. And don't even think about going to the police with this. If you do, I'll find out, and you'll never see your children again.'

The line goes dead then, but that doesn't stop me shouting Nancy's name several times into my phone until I give up because she's definitely gone. I try calling her back, but there is no answer, and it's clear she has nothing more to say to me. She's told me exactly what I need to do, and there is nothing else to it. I know what has to happen next. I know what she expects.

The problem is, Jack doesn't.

I think about calling him and telling him exactly what I've just been told because he obviously has a right to know. Our children's kidnapper has given her demands and they involve him directly, though he's not going to be very happy when he hears what she wants. It's not something he can willingly give, like money. It's something far more costly than that - something that I know he will struggle to comprehend.

Will Jack be willing to die for our children?

And am I willing to risk telling him he has to, just in case he says no?

My head is spinning as I wander out of Times Square and go back in the direction of the hotel where I ran away from my husband half an hour ago. A lot has happened in that time, far more than Jack could imagine, but before I get back to our room and see him, I have to think carefully about what I say when I do.

Nancy gave me a choice. She said I could kill him to save Maddy and Alex and if I do that, do I need to tell Jack what the plan is? Or do I just kill him without saying a word, denying him the chance to run away and save himself and thus condemn our children to a terrible fate? I've been given what feels like an impossible task, but it'll only get more difficult the more Jack knows.

He'll try to talk me out of it. Say there must be another way. Come up with a plan. But all of that will only increase the risk Nancy poses to our children, and I can't have that. That's why I feel like I can't tell Jack what Nancy wants.

So what do I do? I just kill him? *As if it's that's easy...*

He's the father of my children. The man I married. The man I love. The man I was willing to keep a dark secret for over the last fifteen years. The man who ran through fire to save us all.

How am I supposed to just end his life after the history we have together?

But if I tell him what Nancy wants, then maybe I don't have to. Maybe he's not the coward she thinks he is. Maybe Jack will take his own life to save his kids and save me the burden of taking it for him. Could he do that? Could he just take himself away somewhere and commit suicide? Slash his wrists? Jump on a subway line as a train arrives into the station? Jump into the freezing cold water in the harbour and sink to the bottom?

If Bob could do it, maybe Jack can too, though these are very different circumstances.

Bob did it because he was depressed.

Jack would have to do it simply to save someone else.

I feel just as sick at the thought of Jack killing himself as I do at the thought of killing him myself, and by the time I make it back to the hotel, I feel like I could collapse into the bellhop's arms and start weeping. But I don't do that. I just walk straight past him, and after he has held the door open for me, I enter the lobby and make my way to the elevators.

Pushing the button for my floor and watching it light up as the lift shaft whirrs into life, I think about how Jack will probably be pleased to see me when I walk into our room in just a few moments' time. He'll ask where I have been, but without the presence of any police officers with me, he will feel reassured that I haven't gone and told anybody what he did to Conrad in 2008. But he'll surely detect that all is not well with me, and while he might put my low mood down to my worries over Maddy and Alex, he won't really know what I'm thinking about.

He won't know that all I have to do is end his life and our children will be sent back to me.

I get off the elevator and slowly walk towards my hotel room door, my legs feeling heavier with each step I take. My arms are like dead weights too, and it's actually an effort to use my key card to access the room. But once the door opens, I step inside and take a deep breath because this is the moment of truth. I'm about to see Jack, and then I'll know for sure whether or not I can tell him what Nancy wants or whether I'll keep it to myself and wait for my perfect moment to strike.

But there's one more unexpected thing to happen to me this morning.

The room is empty.

Jack is not here.

And if he's not here, how can I do what Nancy wants me to do before it's too late?

23

JACK

The taxi I'm in is struggling just as much as every other vehicle on this road to get to its destination, but slowly but surely, the traffic ahead of us moves forward, and we get a little closer.

The man at the wheel stinks of cigarettes and has spent the last ten minutes telling me all about what he would do to improve the roads in this city if he was mayor. But I've been paying him little attention because my thoughts are focused on the person I am going to see rather than the person who is driving me there.

After realising that Lorna had fled the hotel and was refusing to answer my calls to tell me where she had gone or what she was doing, I had a sinking feeling in my stomach that what I did to Conrad was soon going to become public knowledge. But if that was the case and there was little I could do to stop it, I had to do something other than sit around at the hotel and wait for the police to turn up with their handcuffs and questions.

If Lorna was right and the person behind Maddy and Alex's disappearance was connected to the Williamson family, then I was not going to let them get away with it. But I had to act quickly, just in case I was about to be taken into police custody after Lorna's potentially imminent confessions, so I hailed a cab and here I am, edging my way out of the city.

Our destination is 4275 Claremont Avenue, Stamford, which is the address of the Williamson family home. I know that because it was easy information to find out once I'd heard all about the family in the news during the initial reports of what had happened to their late son, as well as during his parents' numerous public appeals for information in the days that followed. I know they still live there now, or at least Nancy does, thanks to a quick Google search just before I hopped in this cab. There was a news article the other day in which Nancy Williamson was present at the opening of a new library - one her family had helped fund - and she was listed as a resident of Claremont Avenue, which seems like the same address to me.

While I've never been in any way tempted to go to their house before, things have changed now because if that family have taken revenge by kidnapping the children belonging to who they think hurt Conrad, there is a good chance they might be at that house. Or if not, there might at least be somebody there who knows where they are.

My driver warned me that it was going to cost me over $100 to take me to Stamford, but I told him that wasn't a problem, and it's true.

The money is not the problem.

What happens when I get to the house is.

I'm not exactly sure how I am going to approach things when I arrive, but with time of the essence and Maddy and Alex needing somebody to help them, if they are even still alive, then I have no choice but to be bold and get straight to the point. I'll knock on the door and ask whoever answers it if they know anything about what is going on with my kids, and depending on what answer I get, I should be able to at least get a good idea whether I am on the right track or if I've just made another huge mistake.

Thinking of huge mistakes, my stomach lurches again when I think of Lorna and what she might be doing at the moment. For all I know, she could be thirty minutes into a very serious discussion with a detective, and there may already be police officers taking the elevator up to our floor, hoping to find me in our room and catch me completely unaware as they make their arrest. But then I hear my phone ringing, and when I see that it is my wife calling me, I suddenly get hope that she might not have gone to the police yet.

'Lorna?' I say as my driver glances in his rear-view mirror at me on the phone in the back seat and has no choice but to stop his chuntering about the state of New York.

'Jack. Where are you?'

'Where are you? Why did you leave the room without telling me?'

'I had to go for a walk. I needed to clear my head.'

'I was worried about you. I didn't know what you were doing.'

'I'm fine.'

It's funny because while Lorna says that, I can detect in her voice that it is not true.

'Where are you?' she asks me again.

'I'm in a taxi.'

'What? Where are you going?'

I pause because I'm not sure if telling her is a good idea. But then I decide to go ahead and do so because it might help me if she knows I'm looking into her theory that the Williamson family have Maddy and Alex. If she thinks I have a chance of finding them, she may be less likely to speak to the police about Conrad.

'I'm going to see Nancy Williamson,' I say.

'What?'

'If she has anything to do with Maddy and Alex being taken, then I am going to find out and get them back.'

'Wait, you can't do that!'

'Why not? What else can we do? Sit around and wait for the police to find something? That doesn't seem to be working.'

'No, Jack. Do not go there.'

'Why not? You're the one who told me you think they are getting their revenge, so why wouldn't I go?'

'Because I just spoke to Nancy!'

I pause because I'm not quite sure I just heard Lorna correctly.

'What?'

'I spoke to her. She phoned me.'

'When?'

'Just now, while I was out walking.'

'How the hell did she get your number?'

'I guess from Maddy or Alex's phone.'

My heart skips a beat.

'So she does have them?'

'Yes,' comes the chilling reply.

'Speed up,' I say to the driver as I lean forward in my seat. 'I'll give you another hundred dollars if you get me there quicker.'

'I'd love to take your money, man, but I'm going as quick as I can in this traffic,' he replies, throwing up his hands in exasperation as we hit yet another wall of stationary vehicles ahead of us.

'Just try!' I say as I sit back in my seat before putting the phone back to my ear. 'Lorna, I'll be at Nancy's house soon.'

'No, Jack. You can't go there. That's not what she wants.'

'I don't care what she wants. She's got Maddy and Alex! Who the hell does she think she is, taking our kids like this!'

My driver looks very confused now, and I should probably try and calm down a little in case he parks up and tells me to get out. But it must take a lot more than this to dissuade him from making hundreds of dollars because he carries on, leaving me to continue my conversation behind him.

'Have you called the police?' I ask Lorna as we start moving again.

'No, she told me no police!'

'What else did she say?'

There's a pause then.

'Lorna?'

'She said it was Bob who started that fire at our house.'

'What?'

171

I can't believe what she just said, but she confirms it by telling me Nancy told her about her late ex-husband flying to England intent on revenge, though, fortunately for us, he failed.

'That son of a bitch,' I say before I grit my teeth and wonder how he could have started a fire at a house with four people inside. Then again, he most likely wondered how a person could hit his son and drive away, so best not to dwell on that.

'Jack, please. Just come back to the hotel and then we can talk about this.'

I ignore that request before asking Lorna if Nancy made any requests.

'What does she want? It can't be money, can it?' I say, and Lorna confirms that it is not.

'So what is it? Does she want me to go to the police?'

I expect that to be it, but surprisingly, Lorna says no again.

'So what is it?'

'Come back and I'll tell you.'

'Are you kidding? I'm not coming back. That woman has our kids, and I'm going to get them.'

'Jack!'

'No, this has to end, and I am going to end it.'

It might just be all the adrenaline running through my body that causes me to end the call then and urge the driver to put his foot down, but I temporarily forget about Lorna and put all my focus now on finding Nancy.

I know what I did to that woman was wrong, but what she is doing here is wrong too.

Now it's finally time to make things right.

24

LORNA

I've tried calling Jack back, but he isn't picking up his phone anymore. The last thing he told me was that he was going to finish this, so I guess he is still on his way to Nancy's house.

But what will happen when he gets there?

Will she be there? Is that where Maddy and Alex are? Or are they all elsewhere? And what will Nancy do if she finds out that instead of me doing as she wishes and killing Jack, he is running around the city on a one-man mission?

She'll know I've not followed her orders, and she made it very clear what would happen if I didn't.

I'll never see Maddy and Alex again.

I'm desperate for Jack to pick up his phone and give me another chance to convince him to come back to the hotel but after trying him again, he still isn't answering.

Frustrated, I throw my phone down onto the bed and look around helplessly at our suitcases and our numerous items of clothing strewn around the floor. This room is a mess and almost a representation in the real world of what my thoughts feel like in my mind.

Cluttered. Disorganised. *Stressful.*

But then, one clear thought comes to my mind to tell me what I should do next. I should call Nancy and tell her what my husband is doing. That way, I can make it clear that I am not a part of his plan and that anything he does is going against what I have told him to do.

I pick up my phone again and try the number Nancy contacted me on earlier. But to my dismay, it says the number is no longer in service. I guess that is by design, and she made sure I couldn't reach her again just in case I gave the number to the police and they could track her down by using it. But I haven't gone to the police; I'm just trying to talk to her myself. Mother to mother. But I have no way of doing so, and that means I can't tell her that my husband has gone off the grid in a desperate attempt to foil her plot and ruin her plans for revenge.

It feels very strange not to be on my husband's side and as if I have to apologise for his behaviour to the woman who kidnapped our children, but that's what I feel I have to do because I can't have Nancy thinking I didn't take her warning seriously. I'm still not sure exactly what I would have done if Jack had been in this hotel room when I got back because I don't know if I could have killed him like I'm supposed to, but I didn't even get the chance to find out. Jack has almost decided what happens next for me and in some ways, it's similar to how this all began when I came home and found him drinking in our kitchen in the middle of the day.

As much as I love my husband and am grateful for the children we raised together, as well as how he so heroically saved those children from the house fire that I now know was arson, there is no doubt he has a habit of acting selfishly, and I always seem to be the one who is hurt the most. Is that all I am to him - collateral damage?

When will he ever stop and listen to me for a moment instead of simply telling me what he wants to do and leaving me with no choice but to go along with it?

I could have been more forceful back in 2008 and not let him decide what we did next, but he got his way then, and he is getting his way now. The problem is, Jack's way tends to be the one that results in the most pain and destruction, not just for me but for others, and while last time it was me, Conrad and his poor family who suffered, now things have gone up a notch because Maddy and Alex are in the line of fire too.

How can he be acting so selfishly when our children need him to do the right thing? I shouldn't have even had to tell him about going to the police and confessing because he should have been the one suggesting it. He should be taking the simplest course of action to get our kids back but instead, he is taking the selfish course once again, and in this case, it means him thinking he can somehow swoop into Nancy's residence and rescue the kids and leave without anybody knowing why they were taken in the first place.

It's funny, but the longer I stand here in this messy hotel room and think about my husband's self-centred ways, the more I get angry at him, and the angrier I get, the more I feel like I could do what Nancy told me to do. If I was with him right now, maybe I could hurt him - not just because it's what Nancy wants but because it would mean he can't go on and hurt any more people. But I'm not with him, and while he's running around the city, there is no limit to what bad things might happen next. But I know one thing for sure. Whatever happens, it won't be him who suffers the most.

It'll be me.

That's why I have to get to him and stop him before he makes this a whole lot worse.

Remembering that Jack told me how he easily found the Williamsons' address online in the past, I use my phone to conduct an internet search to get that same information. I've never spent much time looking into any news stories about the Williamsons, simply because my levels of guilt were already high enough and doing so would surely only make it worse. But I need to know where they live now so I can potentially intercept Jack and stop him from making what might be a huge mistake on our children's behalf, so I scour the internet for their address.

It takes me a little while, but I eventually find a few references to a Claremont Avenue in Stamford and assume that is where Jack has gone. Looking at the map on my phone, it tells me it is an hour away from here and must be the kind of place a wealthy family like the Williamsons might live. I'm guessing it is a prestigious place, kind of like Oxford and Cambridge are back in England. I can also see on this map that it is very close to Greenwich, the place where Jack hit Conrad with his car, so it makes sense that his family would have lived near there.

From what I know about poor Conrad, he had been skipping school that fateful day when he was killed. If only he had stayed where he was supposed to be, he would never have crossed paths with my husband. But he was in the wrong place at the wrong time, just like Jack was, and after that unlucky set of circumstances, here I am now, fifteen years later, standing alone and panicking in a New York hotel room whilst trying to make it all right again.

With a good lead to go on, I leave the room, intent on hailing the first taxi I see outside this hotel and asking the driver to take me to Stamford. Impatiently pushing the button on the elevator to get it to come to my floor, I am so distracted that when the doors do eventually open, I step in before I've allowed whoever might already be inside to step out.

That's how I end up walking right into a police officer.

'Mrs Thompson,' a voice says as I step back and apologise to the man in the NYPD uniform whom I just bumped into. As I do, I notice another man standing beside him, and he is wearing a suit, which tells me he might be a detective.

'What's happened?' I ask her, fearing they have all come here to give me some bad news about Maddy and Alex. Has Jack already done something stupid and Nancy has retaliated, ruining whatever chance I stood of getting my kids back safe and well?

'We've had a report of a possible sighting of Maddy and Alex,' the man in the suit tells me. 'We need you to come with us right away.'

'Are they okay? Where are they?' I ask. 'Where's Detective Davis?

The cop pushes the button for the ground floor while the detective addresses me.

'Davis is off shift. I'm Detective Freeman. Where is your husband?'

'I don't know,' I reply, lying but deciding to withhold what I do know for the time being in case I only end up making things worse.

He seems puzzled that my partner and I would split up at a time like this, but I don't give him a chance to query that further because I keep bombarding him with questions of my own, questions about Maddy and Alex and whether or not they are alright.

'There has been a report of activity at a warehouse on the outskirts of the city. Two people matching your children's description have been reported being taken inside.'

'So you can get them back?' I cry, hope filling every fibre of my body.

But by the time we make it to the ground floor and step out into the lobby, the detective is being vague with his answers and that worries me.

What does he know that I don't?

Are Maddy and Alex already dead?

25

JACK

As the taxi driver parks up outside the house I've made him drive to, he lets out a loud whistle followed by a couple of comments about how the other half live and how no amount of taxi fares would ever give him the kind of money to be able to afford a place in this neighbourhood. I quickly pay him what I owe, as well as a little extra for him trying his best to get me here as quickly as the traffic allowed, and then I step out on the sidewalk.

Unlike many of the streets back in New York, this one is clean. There are no steaming vents, no bags of rubbish, no graffiti markings, and there are certainly no potholes in the road surface. The residents here clearly expect more from their local council and it looks like they get it.

As the taxi driver departs, no doubt probably still muttering something about all the rich people who live around here, I look at the property before me and take a deep breath.

So this is where the woman who has taken my children lives.

As I'd seen from a street view look on Google Maps, it's a two-storey-tall, stylish, brick build. The lawn is lush and perfectly manicured, and there is a large American flag hanging from a pole by the front door. This is quintessential wealthy suburban America, a home just like many I have seen on TV shows or movies in which the main characters live an aspirational lifestyle. But there's nothing aspirational about what the woman who lives here has been through or done recently, and as I stride towards the house, I am prepared to go in and treat the homeowner how she deserves to be treated.

I won't be overawed by her wealth.

I will simply tell her to give me back what is mine.

Or else.

I hear the wind fluttering the large flag above my head as I reach the front door and lift my hand up to knock. But just before I can, the door opens, and when it does, I see a man with grey hair and a very smart blazer greeting me.

For a second, I wonder if I've gone to the wrong house, but that fear is dispelled when I hear what the man says next.

'Mr Thompson. Do come in, and if you wouldn't mind taking your shoes off, thank you.'

I have no idea who this ultra-polite person is, but he knows my name and has clearly been expecting me. But how? The only person who knew I was coming here was my wife, and she wouldn't have passed that information on to Nancy by way of a warning.
Would she?

'Where is Nancy?' I ask, holding off on stepping inside for the moment. 'Are my children here?'

'Please, come in,' the kindly gentleman says, and now I'm wondering if he is a butler, which would make sense because Nancy certainly has enough money to be able to afford one.

I realise I'm not going to learn much more from out here on the doorstep, so I step inside then, and after the butler has reminded me once again to take off my shoes, I do so before looking around the decadent hallway.

An enormous staircase rises up in front of me, while the walls are adorned with old paintings. But it's the painting in the centre of all the others that my eyes linger on because I recognise who it is in it. It's a portrait of Conrad. Either he posed for it before he died or his family had it commissioned after his death because it looks very similar to how he looked at the age he passed away.

'In here,' the butler says to me, preventing me from staring at the sombre portrait any longer than I have to, and I see he is leading me into another room.

As I follow him in, the first thing I see is a giant fireplace, and while no fire is currently burning, I imagine this is a great place to be in the depths of a frigid winter in this part of the world. But the second thing I see is the top of a head sitting in the chair in front of the fireplace, and now this room has suddenly lost its warm and cosy feeling.

I don't need the person to turn around and look at me to know who it is.

It's her.

Nancy.

'Thank you, Edward,' she says after the butler has delivered the guest to her and as he turns to leave, I hear Nancy order me to take a seat in the vacant armchair beside her. But I stay standing for the time being because I wasn't planning on being here for long.

'Where are my children?' I ask her calmly. 'I know you have them, and I know why you think you had to take them, but this has gone too far. Either you let Maddy and Alex go or I call the police and tell them what you've done.'

'You think I'm afraid of a police officer?' Nancy asks me, and while I still can't fully see her face, I wonder if she might be smirking as she speaks. 'This family has donated over $2 million to the first responders in New York, and I have many friends in the NYPD these days, as I do in the local police force that serves this area around here. So, go ahead, give them a call; I'm sure they'll be happy to come and see me and have a cup of tea. They'll be even happier when I tell them who you are and how you're the key to solving a hit and run case that has been open for fifteen years.'

While I had no intention of calling the police because their being here would be as bad for me as it would be for Nancy, hearing how confidently she speaks about the police makes me fearful of just how many friends in high places she has. Is this why she has been able to pull off such a brazen thing as taking two British holidaymakers in such public places? She isn't afraid of the law because, for people like her, she is almost above the law.

What if money gets you far more than just a big house around here?

'Sit down,' Nancy tells me again, and without any better option, I do as she says, easing myself tentatively into the armchair beside her. Once I have, she finally turns to look at me and while she says nothing as she does, the way her eyes regard me makes me feel utterly awful.

I'm staring into the eyes of the mother whose son I killed, and she is looking at me like she knows exactly who I am and what I have done in my life. Without saying another word, she is making me feel dirty, deceitful, dishonest and downright disgusting. But she isn't making me feel any different to how I've made myself feel plenty of times in the past.

'You want to see your children again,' Nancy says, stating the obvious, and I nod my head, hopeful she is going to give me what I want. 'Well, so do I. I want Conrad to walk through that door and give me a hug. But that's not going to happen, is it? It's not going to happen because you took him from me.'

I could deny that or say any one of a million other things to try and preserve my self-respect, but the look Nancy is giving me is as if she can see into my soul, and I realise that it is utterly pointless to try and sit here and say I'm innocent. I know I'm not and she knows it too, so it would just be a waste of time.

'I'm sorry,' I say, and while my heart is racing because my body knows I'm confessing my deepest sin to somebody other than my wife for the first time ever, I forge on anyway. 'It was an accident. I'm so, so sorry.'

Nancy is not surprised by my admission, nor does she accept my apology, not that I expected her to.

She doesn't even look sympathetic at how tormented I clearly am by what happened in the past. She just keeps staring at me and making me feel even smaller than I am.

'Tell me what happened,' Nancy demands, and after having her assure me that I will see my children again if I do, I run through it all. But unlike with Lorna, when I gave her numerous excuses as to why I wasn't fully concentrating on the road that day when Conrad stepped out in front of my car, I just keep it simple. I don't try to excuse what I did by blaming it on any number of things that make it seem like I was just unlucky. I give it to Nancy straight because she deserves to hear the truth.

I was just not concentrating and because of that, a thirteen-year-old boy lost his life and is never coming home again.

While it's not exactly a relief to sit here and get it all off my chest, I do hope that Nancy feels at least 1% better now than she did five minutes ago. If I've eased her pain even in the slightest, then I suppose that is something, but now that I have tried my best to do that, I need her to want to return the favour.

'Where are Maddy and Alex?' I ask her.

Nancy wipes away a tear from her eye after hearing my account of Conrad's death before she calls out for Edward, the butler.

'They're at a warehouse outside New York,' she tells me just before Edward enters the room looking eager to be of service again. Once he's here, Nancy gives him an order.

'Get my car ready,' she tells him. 'Jack and I are going for a drive.'

26

LORNA

I'm being driven in a police car alongside the detective who came to tell me that there had been a reported sighting of Maddy and Alex at a warehouse outside the city, and as I look out of the window, I see the skyscrapers growing smaller in the distance. It looks like we are now passing through an impoverished part of New York, a place far away from the tourist attractions where the cameras flash, and into a place that definitely does not feature in any holiday brochures which might be trying to entice people from a foreign land to come here and experience a slice of the Big Apple.

There are abandoned buildings on both sides of the street, many with broken windows or missing front doors, and as we move on into an industrial estate, I see warehouses that look to be in as much disrepair as the buildings we passed on the way to get here.

While this is not a nice place to be, it does look like the perfect place to hide a couple of people who have been taken from their parents because it's far enough away from where anybody might see.

But somebody did see. Detective Freeman has told me a member of the public who was out here walking their dog made a 911 call to report seeing two people, one male and one female, who appeared to be aged in their early twenties or late teens being bundled out of a car and pushed inside a warehouse before the door was closed behind them. Suspecting that was a little odd, the police were informed and now we are on the way to investigate. Detective Freeman came to pick me up in case I can be useful in whatever situation we are about to enter into because, as of yet, we don't know if there will be a need for negotiating to get the hostages released.

We also don't know if we're already too late to save those hostages.

But I guess we're just about to find out.

'Park here - we don't want to get too close,' Freeman says, and the officer at the wheel brings us to a stop beside one of the many dilapidated warehouses around here.

I sit forward in my seat, wondering if the warehouse in question is just around the corner from here. That must be where the rest of the police officers are, presumably having cordoned off the area. But then again, they may not want to spook the people inside the warehouse because if whoever has Maddy and Alex gets spooked, be it Nancy or a group of people she has employed, then this might not end well. But sitting here when I could be potentially so close to my children is unbearable, and I feel like I have to do something. That's why I ask the officer what the plan is.

But I do not get a good answer.

'Get out of the car,' Freeman says as the officer in the front turns and points his gun right at me.

'What are you doing?' I ask him as I stare at the firearm, but the penny hasn't dropped yet. But it does when Detective Freeman tells me again that I am to get out of the car, and the fact he isn't admonishing his colleague for brandishing his weapon tells me this is all part of whatever their plan is.

And their plan is clearly different to mine.

'Wait,' I say, but it's hard to get my own way with a gun on me, and it becomes even harder when the detective tells me he doesn't want to hurt me but he will if I don't comply. That's why I have no choice but to follow his orders and as I do, the officer and his gun match my movements, meaning there's not even the slimmest of chances for me to make a run for it now.

'Why are you doing this? What's going on?' I ask the detective as he joins us outside the vehicle, but he just points to the way he wants me to start walking.

'I thought you were helping me! Where are my kids?' I ask, panicking because surely this can't be happening. Why are these men not helping me find Maddy and Alex like they should be doing? Why does it seem like they're working with Nancy rather than against her?

'Tell me where you are taking me!' I cry, but when I stop walking, I feel the end of the gun burrowing into my back and that forces me to carry on again.

As we walk around a corner, I do not see several other police officers all waiting outside a warehouse to storm inside and rescue my children as I was hoping. Instead, there's nobody out here but the three of us, and as the detective leads us to a door at the front of one of the many disused buildings around here, I am starting to worry that nobody else is going to come here.

'Are you going to kill me?' I ask just before I enter the building, but again, the gun has a powerful way of making me keep moving, and I'm forced to go inside. When I do, the detective tells me to go and stand in the middle of this large and otherwise empty room we are in.

'Why? What are you going to do to me?' I ask as I realise my children are not here and this has all been a trap.

'Just go,' the detective says with a heavy sigh as if he isn't getting paid enough for putting up with me and my objections. But I've had enough of being manipulated by him and his colleague's gun, so I stand my ground and ask them again what is going to happen, and surprisingly, I get an answer this time.

'We're going to wait here until your husband arrives,' the detective tells me. 'And then this will all be over.'

27

LORNA

I don't know exactly how long we waited, but eventually, the detective was right, and my husband arrived to join me at this warehouse. But also, like me, he had been brought here under false pretences and as he entered the warehouse to see a police officer pointing a gun at me, he understandably panicked. But he soon shut up when the gun was turned on him, and as Nancy entered the warehouse behind him, she acted like this was all part of her plan and it had gone just the way it should have done.

'What's going on?' Jack asks, seeking the answer to a question that was just on the tip of my tongue when I saw Nancy enter.

'Go over there and join your wife,' Nancy tells him, and while Jack momentarily stalls and asks all the things I've asked, the gun makes him comply like it made me comply, too.

'Are you okay?' he asks as he reaches me, and I nod my head to let him know I haven't been hurt, at least not yet anyway. He looks physically unharmed as well, but he's obviously as confused as I am, and with neither of us having any answers yet, we both look to Nancy to get some.

And finally, she enlightens us.

'I wasn't expecting you to pay me a visit, Jack, but I'm glad you did,' she begins as the detective and the police officer stand by idly, confirming they are mere pawns in her game rather than actual upstanding custodians of the law in this city. 'That's because it should make what I want to happen even easier. Isn't that right, Lorna?'

I'm not quite on Nancy's wavelength, nor is my husband.

'What are you talking about?' Jack asks her.

'I'm talking about what I have asked your wife to do for me,' Nancy says, appearing calm, but I'm anything but now that she has brought up the awful ultimatum that she gave to me earlier.

Jack is looking at me too, very confused, as he well might be, because it's obvious there is more going on here than he has been party to. But what can I do? Tell him I am supposed to kill him to save the kids?

'I have asked Lorna to kill you,' Nancy says, completely shattering any hope I might have had about keeping that fact quiet.

'What?'

Jack looks mortified and now he looks at me not out of love, but out of trepidation.

'That's right,' Nancy goes on, seemingly enjoying this. 'I'm aware it's quite a bold request but the thing is, you dying is the only way I can punish you how I would like, and making Lorna do it is the only way I can punish her for her role in all of this too.'

'You're crazy,' Jack scoffs. 'Why the hell would my wife kill me?'

'Because she wants to see Maddy and Alex again,' comes the simple response, and now Jack realises this might not be as crazy as he first thought.

'Wait, Lorna, you're not entertaining this madness, are you?' he asks me nervously.

'No, of course not,' I say, but I did hesitate, and everyone in this big, cold and empty room noticed it.

'I told Lorna what I wanted when we spoke earlier, and I expected her to carry out my wishes to save her children,' Nancy says. 'But when I was told that you were on your way to me by the people I had watching you in New York, I figured I might as well bring you together to save time. That's why I enlisted the help of a couple of my friends in the NYPD to bring you here, Lorna, and now that you have been reunited, this should all be over much quicker than I imagine it would have been if I'd left you two to it.'

Jack laughs as if this is all one big joke but sadly for everyone involved, it is not. But while he's doing that, I am looking at the two 'friends in the NYPD' that Nancy just referred to. It's confirmation, not that I needed it, that these two rogue cops are on her payroll and shows how she really does have friends in high places who are willing to help her get her revenge.

'Wait, I thought you said the police let you down over the investigation into Conrad's death?' I ask her, referring to our earlier conversation when she told me the police didn't pay much attention to her suggesting Jack was the potential culprit of the unsolved hit and run.

'I did,' Nancy confirms. 'That's why I realised it was far better to have friends in the force than not. What's the easiest way to make friends? Buy them.'

I shake my head as I wonder just how many other people there are in New York and the surrounding areas who have been helping this wealthy woman today too, but all that matters is that Jack and I are clearly no match for the kind of power she wields. I guess that explains how Nancy is so confident that she is going to get away with all this.

The kidnapping. Bringing me to this warehouse at gunpoint. And the potential of Jack's body having to be disposed of. They are all serious crimes, but why should the person who has carried them all out be worried about facing the law when the police are already on her side?

The only ones here who have anything to worry about are me and Jack.

'We are going to leave you with a gun,' Nancy says. 'And it will have to be used if Maddy and Alex are to be saved. Lorna, either you shoot your husband or you shoot yourself, Jack. Either way, I want you dead,' she says, pointing a finger in the direction of my husband. 'And I want you, Lorna, to suffer for this by becoming a widow like I am,' she says, moving her finger in my direction now. 'We will wait outside while you do what you have to do, and I will only return with the information on the whereabouts of Maddy and Alex if two things happen. One, we hear a gunshot and two, we know Jack is dead.'

With that, Nancy, the detective and the police officer head for the door, but just before they walk out, the detective reveals a gun, and he wipes it down with a cloth before placing it on the concrete floor. It's obvious that it is supposed to be the gun I am to use to kill Jack but while my husband protests, I just stare at it until the three of them have left the warehouse, and now, only two of us remain in here.

It's just me and Jack.

Husband and wife.

But two have to become one.

28

JACK

I'm waiting for the part when my wife tells me that she is not even contemplating what Nancy has told her to do and will console me and say we'll get through this together instead. But that's not happening. Lorna is not saying a word.

All she is doing is staring at that gun.

Neither one of us has gone anywhere near it since it was left here for us by that unscrupulous detective, but according to Nancy, this will only end when that gun is used to end my life. But unfortunately for her, I cannot see a world in which she gets what she wants because I'm not dying here today.

Am I?

'Lorna, what is going on? She phoned you and told you to kill me? Why didn't you tell me?'

'I was going to tell you, but you weren't at the hotel. You'd gone to see Nancy.'

'We spoke on the phone. You could have mentioned it!'

'I know. I'm sorry,' Lorna says, her eyes still on the gun.

'This is stupid. We just need to walk out of here together,' I say, and I take my wife's hand and plan to lead her to the door in the hope that the pair of us can walk straight past that gun on the way out. Or maybe I'll pick it up and use it to fight my way out of here should I meet any resistance from those outside. But no sooner have I touched Lorna's hand than she pulls it away from me, and that does not give me confidence that she is on my side here as much as I thought she would be.

'Hey, what's wrong?'

'You know what's wrong,' she replies quietly. 'Maddy and Alex won't be safe unless we do what Nancy wants.'

I laugh then because I simply can't help it. But Lorna isn't laughing.

'Wait, you're not seriously saying I have to die, are you?'

'It's the only way she'll let them go!'

'How do you know that?' I cry. 'She could be lying! You might be arrested for my murder, and then the kids will have no one even if she does let them go!'

'No, she wouldn't do that.'

'How do you know?'

'I just do!'

'Oh my God.'

I stare at Lorna in disbelief, but even though I am shocked, it's just as scary because I know she is right. If this is the only way to ensure Maddy and Alex's survival, then what choice do we have? And what choice would a good parent have? Most parents would sacrifice themselves to save their children, but how often is that put to the test? People say and think it, but it's usually whilst safe in the knowledge that such a thing is unlikely to ever happen.

Just like them, I've always thought I'd be willing to die for my kids.

But I never actually thought I'd literally have to do so.

It's a good job we're in a cavernous warehouse because I need a lot of space to think, and I step away from Lorna then and begin pacing around, racking my brains for any way in which this doesn't have to be the end of everything. With my hands on my head and an awful sinking feeling in my stomach, I try to conceive of a world in which I can reason with Nancy and make her see that she doesn't want to do this. My death will be on her conscience forever, and surely, she won't want to live with that, will she? But I already know the answer to that one and it's not an optimistic one.

But what about Lorna? Could she live with it on her conscience too? She is supposed to kill me, but I doubt she will actually be able to pull the trigger. It's more likely that I'd have to pull it myself, taking my own life to give Nancy what she wants.

But can I do it?

Do I want to do it?

'This isn't about us; it's about Maddy and Alex,' Lorna says to me as she watches me pacing around. 'They are the only innocent ones here. They didn't kill Conrad, and they didn't cover it up. We did. We're guilty, and that's why we have to be punished. But not them. They don't deserve this. I just want them to be safe.'

'In what world is me dying not punishing the kids?' I ask. 'They'll lose their father!'

That shuts Lorna up for a minute, so I double down on this line of persuasion.

'We're a family. We stick together. I don't want to lose them, and I'm sure they don't want to lose me either. So there has to be another way.'

'No, stop it! You don't get to do this! Not again!'

I stop pacing when I hear Lorna's outburst.

'What do you mean?' I ask her nervously.

'I mean you talking me into doing something I don't want to do, like you did with Conrad. Can't you see? You are never willing to take responsibility for your actions and because of that, everyone else in your family has to suffer!'

'Am I not suffering too?' I cry. 'I'm missing Maddy and Alex, and I'm apparently supposed to die in here today, so in what way am I not suffering?'

'Are you stupid? You deserve to suffer! You killed that boy! I didn't do it, neither did Maddy and Alex. So why are we the ones who have to pay? Take some responsibility for leaving that boy by the roadside!'

By the sounds of it, Lorna has just released fifteen years of pent-up frustration. But that's not the scariest part. That would be the realisation I've just come to.

It's the realisation that, for the first time ever in our marriage, my wife is no longer on my side.

'You're actually entertaining the idea of killing me?' I ask, utterly aghast.

'Yes. I mean no! I don't know!' Lorna cries, clearly confused.

'Which one is it? I have a right to know!'

'Just shut up! Please, stop talking. I need to think.'

'No, this has gone too far now,' I say, and I walk towards the gun, ready to pick it up.

'What are you doing?' Lorna asks me, but I'm not sure myself, so I don't answer her. But as I pick the gun up, holding it as tentatively as a person who has never held a gun before would do, I suddenly lose all the fight in me. Instead of wanting to debate this with my wife now, I feel the helplessness of my situation wash over me, and Lorna is not the only one with tears in her eyes.

'Jack,' Lorna says when she sees the change in me, but I just shake my head because I don't want us to argue anymore.

'You're right,' I say, hating myself as much as I've ever done before because I only now can see how truly selfish I have been in my life. 'What I made you do back then wasn't fair. Keeping it secret for me. That was wrong. I should never have put you in that position. And what is happening to Maddy and Alex now isn't fair either.'

The gun is shaking in my trembling hand.

'Jack.'

'No, let me finish,' I say. 'I should have owned up to what I did. I should have gone to prison. I'd have been out by now and we'd all have been safe. That's what you told me to do back in '08, but I didn't listen to you. I thought I could handle this all myself, but the truth is, it was never just about me. It was about Nancy and her family and mine too. I've ruined so many lives with what I've done.'

I look down at the gun then and wonder if using it is really the best thing to do here. Not only would it potentially save my children, but it would also put me out of my misery. I wouldn't have to wake up every morning and have Conrad Williamson's dead body be the first thought on my mind, just like I wouldn't have to look in the mirror every day and see the face of a killer and a liar looking back at me. This might be what Nancy wants, but could it end up being what I want too?

A way out? A chance to truly avoid prison? A chance to avoid many more years of guilt?

Just pull the trigger, Jack, and it'll all be over, and with that, it'll be over for everyone else, too.

'Jack,' Lorna says for a third time before she reaches me and takes hold of my arm, the one with the gun at the end of it, and presumably, it's to give me pause for thought so she can say what's on her mind. But she doesn't try and talk me out of it. She just tells me how much she loves me, and that only makes this feel even more real as I grip the gun.

Then I do what I should have done a long time ago.

I accept responsibility for my actions.

'I love you so much,' I say to Lorna. 'The kids too. Let them know how much I loved them, okay?'

Lorna is crying too much to answer me, but I've said almost everything that I needed to, and that only leaves me with one more thing to say.

'Turn away. I don't want you to see this.'

Lorna shakes her head as if she is now the one who is against this idea of me dying, but I know it's just going to take her a few more seconds before she is ready.

'If it's the only way to get them back, then this has to happen,' I say, and Lorna nods her head before slowly backing away, still stifling sobs as she goes.

I wait until she has turned around and got a safe distance away from me before I put the gun to my head and take several deep breaths, sucking in the last parts of oxygen I'll ever get. Then I close my hands, and while I feel my hand still shaking, everything else in my world goes still. My thoughts are clear for the first time in a long time.

Just do it. Pull the trigger. Save Maddy and Alex and allow my family to go home safe and well.

More deep breaths.

More shaking.

Be a good dad. Be a good husband. Pay for what you did to Conrad and his family.

Even more deep breaths.

More urges from my frightened mind to just pull this damn trigger.

Then I lower the gun and let out an anguished cry.

I can't do it.

Lorna senses something is wrong because she looks back at me then and when she does, she finds me with my hands on my knees, almost hyperventilating.

'I'm sorry,' I say as she walks back over to me and puts a hand on my shoulder.

'It's okay,' she says, but I know it's just words, not facts, because if Nancy doesn't get what she wants, then it can't be okay. But then Lorna speaks again.

'Give me the gun.'

I look up at her and see that my wife's tears have stopped now, and a very calm expression has come over her face. While I'm floundering, she is having a moment of clarity.

Where I have failed, she plans to succeed.

'Lorna, you don't have to do this; I can do it,' I try, not wanting this on my wife's conscience. But she has clearly seen that I'm unable to do what is necessary, and she easily takes the gun from me, removing it from my weak grip before taking a few steps back to create a little distance between us.

I stare at her with frightened eyes but know better than to make this even harder for her than it already is by trying to beg for my life, so I stay quiet and prepare for the end to come, an end that I should have been man enough to bring about myself but could not.

But despite seeming more confident, Lorna is unable to pull the trigger either and when she lowers the gun like I just did a moment ago, I guess Maddy and Alex can't count on their parents saving them as much as they might have hoped.

'Lorna, it's okay. I-'

That's all I can get out before the gun is raised again, and this time, my wife pulls the trigger.

29

LORNA

The door to the warehouse opens, but I don't look up to see who is coming inside.

I just keep staring at the dead body in front of me.

The body of my husband.

'I'll take that,' the man beside me says, 'and as Detective Freeman relieves me of the gun, Nancy stands over Jack and looks down on him, no doubt to check that he is really dead. But the detective checks for a pulse just to make sure, and once he confirms what I already knew, Nancy turns away from him and looks at me.

'Thank you,' is all she has to say.

'Where are Maddy and Alex?' I ask her, making it clear exactly why I just did such a heinous thing.

'A deal is a deal. I'll take you to your children now, and you can all go home,' Nancy says.

'What about my husband?' I ask, unsure of what happens with him and afraid that he might just be left here on the floor of this warehouse for an awfully long time.

'He'll be taken away,' Nancy says, nodding towards the detective and the police officer, who are surely adept enough to know how to dispose of a body without it being found. But while that's hardly comforting, something else troubles me too.

'How am I supposed to get away with this?' I ask. 'People will know Jack is missing. They'll ask me what happened. What am I supposed to tell them?'

'You tell them the truth about what he did,' Nancy replies calmly. 'You tell him that he confessed to you that he was the one who killed Conrad Williamson and that with his guilt having become too much while he was back in New York, he disappeared. That's as much as you know.'

'And you think people will buy that?'

'I don't care. That's what you will tell them.'

'But then the police might be looking at you if I say Jack killed your son.'

'Don't worry about me, I'll be fine there,' Nancy says, and I have to believe that considering she already has two members of law enforcement helping her pull off this deadly scheme.

But while she doesn't seem to be worried about how she might fare if faced with any questions from the police, I can't say the same for myself.

'What if they make me a suspect in Jack's disappearance?' I ask. 'What if they question me and think I'm lying?'

'Then you better make sure you are convincing,' Nancy says cooly. 'Your children are going to need you, and you won't be much use to them if you're locked up in a New York prison, will you?'

My children. My heart breaks for Maddy and Alex as I stare at their father's body and think about how they will never see him again, nor can they ever know the full story of what happened in his last few moments.

They can't know that he was murdered or that I was the one who pulled the trigger because that would destroy them. But what's the alternative? Tell them that their father just walked away and ended his life? He abandoned them? Would they believe that? If so, surely that will destroy them in a different way.

'Time to go,' Nancy tells me before I have more time to think about the dreadful situation I'm in. Even with Jack dead and my kids seemingly saved, I know this isn't over. But the only way I can get my feet moving to the door is to tell myself to take one thing at a time, and I also have to ensure that Jack did not die in vain. He lost his life to save our children, so they have to be the priority now, and thankfully, Nancy is honouring her word, so at least I don't have to worry about them coming to harm anymore.

But leaving the warehouse is not easy because it means leaving Jack too, and I feel sick when I glance back and see the detective and the police officer already beginning the preparations for the removal of his body. I imagine they will be putting him in the trunk of their car before taking him away to a pre-determined site where he will be buried - a site where they will expect him to remain undiscovered for a very long time.

While I knew pulling the trigger on that gun would ensure that Jack would never be coming back home to England with us, I'm hit with an awful sickly feeling when I imagine getting on that plane from JFK soon and leaving my husband behind here. New York is so far from where we live, but this is to be Jack's final resting place. He won't have a proper grave near our house, one I can visit on a regular basis with a bunch of flowers and a few words to say, hoping he might be able to hear me even though he's gone. He's across an entire ocean, and what's more, I won't even know exactly which part of New York he is buried in. I'll just be left with a very vague idea of what I imagine his final resting place to be, and that's all I'll have to think about on that long flight home, as well as on all the long, lonely nights when I'm lying in bed by myself in the years to come.

The only way I think I can bear this is to tell myself that he died heroically for Maddy and Alex. The only way I can handle the guilt of killing him is also to remind myself of just what was at stake if I didn't do it. Now it's done, Maddy and Alex have their chance at a future Jack already lived. They can get married and have children. They can build careers and buy a home. And they can know what it feels like to be willing to do anything for the sake of their family, even if it means doing something terrible to save them.

The fresh air is of no relief to me as I follow Nancy away from the warehouse and towards her waiting car. Her driver opens the door for her and I am told to get in the back alongside her, which I do. Then, with us both on the backseat, we start driving.

I stare out of the window as we leave this industrial estate behind, a much unloved part of the city that has surely seen some unsavoury things during its time, due to its location and the lack of a strong police presence in these parts. Now there is one more unsavoury thing to add to that list. Another body.

Another crime. Another thing that shouldn't have happened but has.

As we leave the warehouses behind, we move onto a road that runs alongside a river, and I know it is the Hudson. I can also see the tall buildings of the city across the large expanse of water, and over there is where all the tourists will be enjoying themselves. But I'm over here, hating myself, my life and this city, and all I want to do is get away from this place.

This time, I mean it when I say I will never come back.

'How far is it?' I ask Nancy when the silence in the car has become almost unbearable.

'Not far,' she says, but I'm surprised at just how much she meant that when the car is brought to a stop a moment later.

Looking around the vehicle, I cannot see anywhere that might be housing Maddy and Alex. All I can see is the river on one side of the car and a desolate wasteland of concrete on the other, where I presume a few old buildings used to stand, but they have now been demolished and nothing has been rebuilt on their foundations yet.

What's going on?

'Okay, Lorna. Time to get out of the car,' Nancy says and when I look at her, I see that she is pointing a gun at me.

That's when I realise that I have been lied to.

'No, wait. You can't do this! I did what I was asked to do!' I cry, but those appeals fall on deaf ears as the door beside me is opened and the driver pulls me out.

'Nancy! Wait! Think about this!' I try as I'm bundled down to the edge of the river, my feet scrabbling over loose rocks as I go.

But it seems like Nancy has done all the thinking she is going to because when I turn back to look at her, with my hands out in front of me in desperation, she has the gun raised towards me.

'Turn around,' she tells me.

'No! You promised me my children would be safe! Why are you doing this?'

I'm not sure if Nancy is even going to do me the decency of giving me an explanation, but thankfully, she does at least give me that, which buys me a little more time.

'There is no way I can let you get away with your part in this,' Nancy tells me. 'No matter how much I might have told myself that I would feel better as long as Jack was dead, I know that you need to die too.'

'Why?'

'Because you're a mother, and that means you know what a cruel thing you did to me by not letting me find out who killed my son! How could you do that to another mother? How could you do that to me?'

'I'm so sorry!' I say as I cry and keep my hands out in front of me, as if they will be enough to stop a bullet. 'I really am! Just let me go, please!'

'Don't you see? I can't let any of you go,' Nancy says coldly. 'All four of you have to die. That's the only way I can definitely get away with this.'

'What? No! Don't kill them! Please!'

'What makes you think your children aren't already dead?'

Nancy's horrifying question causes me to howl in pain, and I lose all my fighting spirit at the thought of Maddy and Alex already being gone.

Nancy tells me to turn around again and despite not wanting to, I know it's either that or stare at the gun as it fires, and that seems worse, so very reluctantly, I turn to face the river, and as I stare out across the murky water, I cannot believe this is the last thing I am ever going to see. But what else can I do? There is no escape. No way for me to get out of this and even if I do, what would be waiting for me to find? The dead bodies of my children?

I don't know if they are even still alive at this point, and maybe I don't want to know.

Maybe I should just give up.

But it's the thought of my children that reminds me of something that might help me here.

I was occasionally glancing at the film Alex was watching on the flight to New York, and while I saw glimpses of various scenes in that action movie, there is one scene that comes back to me most prominently now. It was a scene in which the main character was in a situation very much like the one I find myself in now, where he had an enemy's gun on him and was expected to just stand and prepare to meet his maker. But he didn't just give up and accept his fate. From what I remember in the scene, he fell to the floor before the trigger could be pulled and when his enemy stepped a little closer to investigate what had caused him to fall, or simply to just get a better angle to fire the bullet into his body from, the hero surprised his attacker by throwing sand in their face before leaping to their feet and taking the gun and turning it on them.

It all seemed so unlikely when I was watching it but then again, it was a movie, so there is always a suspension of disbelief with those. But what if I was to try that now? Could it work? It's either that or stand here and wait for the bullet to hit me.

Looking down at my feet, I see numerous rocks of various sizes, and I'm wondering if I could use one of these in much the same way the hero in the film used the sand to disarm his attacker.

It's time to find out.

Before Nancy can discharge her weapon, I allow myself to just flop to the floor, looking limp and lifeless and, hopefully, confusing my attacker. It seems to do the trick because Nancy hasn't fired yet, and when she asks me what I am doing, I make sure to remain still until I hear her walking a little closer. When I feel like there is less of a gap between us, I pick up a rock and roll over quickly before launching it in Nancy's direction, and while my throw misses her, the rock whizzing past her head does enough to temporarily distract her.

Leaping to my feet, I rush at her and shoulder barge her to the ground, all the anger of her lying to me being released in one whirl of energy, and the gun falls from her hand. Before anybody else can grab it, I pick it up and pull the trigger on a gun for a second time today. *After I have, Nancy is no longer with us.*

But there is still the matter of the man who drove us here, though he doesn't look anywhere near as confident in the presence of a firearm as his former boss did, nor like the detective or police officer who were with us earlier did either. He just looks terrified and begs me not to shoot, but I'm not going to do that. Not yet anyway. That's because he might possess a valuable piece of information I need.

'Are my children dead?' I ask him, well aware that if the answer is a bad one, then I might as well shoot this man and then turn the gun on myself because I won't want to live anyway.

The next word out of this man's mouth will affect his future and mine.

So what is it to be?

Yes?

Or no?

30

MADDY

'Come on!' I cry as I give the heavy door in front of me another kick. But just like all the other times I've tried, it doesn't seem to have any impact. This door, the one thing between me, my brother and our freedom, is not budging, no matter how many times I kick it, or shoulder barge it, or pray for it to be opened from the other side by somebody else.

I don't know how long it's been since anybody last came through it, but it feels like an awfully long time, and despite Alex trying to reassure me that things will be okay, I'm beginning to panic that they won't be.

If this door doesn't open again, then we will starve to death in here.

'Let me have another go,' Alex says, and I step aside to allow my brother to have another opportunity at kicking down this door himself. But just like me, he makes very little progress, and after several more futile attempts, he gives up too.

That's when we move on to Plan B, which involves shouting as loud as we can in the vain hope that somebody out there will hear us and be able to help. But even if whoever is listening is not on our side, it would at least be a relief to know that they were still out there, and maybe they'll come in to see us, if only to tell us to be quiet or else. But our cries go unanswered, making me even more fearful that we have been left in here for good now.

'It's useless,' I say, unable to play the role of the brave elder sibling any longer. I've given up and to make that perfectly clear, I slump down against the wall and start to cry.

'Hey, come on, sis. It's not over yet,' Alex says as he sits down beside me, and it's only his handcuffs that prevent him from putting a comforting arm around my shoulder. I know he would if he could, just like I would try and hug him if I had the chance. But our restraints mean that all we can do is sit shoulder to shoulder on the floor of this damn room and contemplate what appears to be our very grim fate. It's that fact which makes me struggle to stem the flow of my tears, and it would take a lot for my brother to say something powerful enough to get me to stop sobbing and alter my outlook.

But he somehow manages it.

'I'm in love with a guy called James,' Alex says, and I stop crying immediately.

'What?'

'He's in my acting class in Manchester.'

I really don't know what to say to that. It certainly wasn't what I was expecting to hear my brother come out with as we sat here and tried to figure out a way to survive.

'He's not the first guy I've liked in that way. David in my Maths class was. But he's not even the first David I've liked. That would be David Beckham.'

I realise now what my brother is trying to tell me, but the fact he is revealing his sexuality to me at a time like this is a troubling one. I'm not troubled by what he's saying, but more that he must think he is really going to die here if he is willing to reveal something he has obviously wrestled with keeping a secret for so long. That's why I try to break the sombre nature of his big announcement by trying to keep it light.

'Hey, hands off. I saw David Beckham first,' I tell him, and he laughs, which is nice to see. Then I let him know that what he has just said was not something he needed to have spent any time worrying about telling me or anyone else.

'Hey, bro. It doesn't matter if you like guys or girls. I'm still your big sister, and I'll love you whatever,' I say. 'Mum and Dad too.'

I'm speaking the truth, but the look on Alex's face tells me he clearly has spent a lot of time doubting that.

'You really think Dad would be okay with it?' he asks me.

'Are you kidding? He doesn't care about anything like that. He just wants you to be happy.'

Alex still looks a little unsure, but I nod my head to show him it is true.

'Why are you telling me now?' I ask him.

'Just in case we don't get out of here.'

'We are getting out of here.'

'Okay, well, if we do, please don't tell anybody what I just said. Especially James.'

'Fine, but I can't promise I won't tell David Beckham if I see him.'

Alex laughs again.

'But seriously, bro. Just be who you want to be and don't worry what anyone else thinks.'

'I guess.'

Alex goes on to tell me how he has spent a long time not only worrying about his sexuality, but also his career goals.

'Acting is hard. What if I never make it?' he asks me.

'And what if you do?' I fire back. 'And by the way, bro. You're just about to turn eighteen, not eighty, so you've got plenty of time to figure things out.'

'Yeah, I guess I'm not as ancient as you are yet,' Alex says cheekily, and now it's my turn to laugh.

Our conversation, as well as our sibling humour, has led to both of us temporarily forgetting about our predicament, but there's only so long we can put off returning our thoughts to the locked door and what happens if it doesn't open. When we do, I tell Alex that I have a few regrets of my own about how I was living my life on the outside before we ended up trapped in here.

'I cheated on one of my uni exams,' I tell my brother, and he looks shocked when he hears it, as he well might because I've always been something of a perfect student, whether that was at school, at sixth form college or university now. But I'm no longer as perfect as I liked to think, at least not academically anyway.

'There was a guy selling the exam papers at a party one night,' I tell Alex. 'Everyone thought he was joking at first, but it turned out that he did actually have access to them. But nobody said yes, mainly because he was charging so much money to look at them. But I was really tempted because I hadn't been revising hard enough, so I told him I'd pay him when we were alone together. I used what money I had left in my student account then asked Mum and Dad for more, telling them I'd run out because our fridge had broken and ruined all the food I had in there.'

Alex looks at me with a mixture of shock and a little delight; shock because he could never have imagined his sister doing something naughty, but delighted because now he realises he doesn't have to try to live up to what he thought was his perfect sibling who could never do anything wrong.

'I can't believe it. You? Miss goody-two-shoes cheated on an exam?' he says with a chuckle.

'Yeah, but that's not even the worst part,' I say. 'The worst part is even then, I almost failed anyway.'

Alex is really laughing now, and I can't blame him because even I have to find it funny that I still almost messed up on an exam paper that I had already seen the answers to. But it's also something I'm not proud of.

'I wish I hadn't done it. I knew I'd always regret it, even if I did graduate. But I guess it doesn't matter now.'

'We'll get out of here,' Alex says, trying to pick up the mood again, but despite his best efforts, it's obvious why we both just shared things we potentially thought we'd never tell anybody.

We both think this is going to end badly for us.

And then we hear voices on the other side of the door.

'Someone's there,' I say as I scramble to my feet, and after Alex has done the same, the pair of us start shouting again, praying that whoever is outside will come in. I don't even care if it's that woman who put us in here or anyone who works for her. I just want this door to open and for somebody to tell me that we might be let go at some point.

And then the door does open, although it's not as I would have expected it to. Instead of it being unlocked, it is kicked down by a burly police officer, and there is another one just like him right behind him. They enter and see us standing in the middle of the room. But just before I can thank them for saving us, I see another person enter the room.

It's Mum.

'Are you okay?' she asks us as she rushes to us both and checks us for any visible injuries. But we both reassure her that we are fine before asking her the same thing. Then the natural thing is for us to ask where Dad is because he's the only one missing now after we have been rescued and reunited.

But that's when Mum goes quiet.

It's also when the look on her face lets us know this is where the good news ends.

31

LORNA

The tall towers on Manhattan Island are receding from view out of my window, and it sure is good to see them getting smaller as the plane I am a passenger on roars its way out of the city towards the ocean and, eventually, to England. As New York fades away, my thoughts turn to home, or at least the new version of home that will be waiting for me when I get there. That's because things are going to be different now that Jack is no longer with me, and the house is going to feel very empty when Maddy returns to university and Alex is at acting class or just out seeing friends. That's when I'll really feel the void my husband's passing has left in my life. But so far, I've not really had a moment to be by myself since Jack died, and that's for various different reasons.

Number one is that I've not been far from my children ever since I was reunited with them inside the room they had been locked in at Nancy's house. As far as I was concerned, I didn't want to let them out of my sight again once I had found them, and neither Maddy nor Alex wanted to leave me either.

Not once they found out what had happened to their father.

I glance at the two brave souls sitting beside me on this plane and when I do, I see Maddy reading a magazine while Alex is watching a film. The pair of them look content enough at the moment, but I know that appearances are deceiving, and they are both struggling on the inside. And how could they not be after all they have had to not only endure since they came to New York, but also what they have learnt about both their mother and father since then too?

Picking up my plastic cup and taking a long gulp of the gin and tonic concoction that is in there, a concoction made up for me by one of the members of the cabin crew, I think about everything that unfolded shortly after Jack's demise. The most dramatic part was undoubtedly me surviving Nancy and her desire to shoot me and presumably push my body into the Hudson, where it might never have been found again. I know I was extremely lucky to avoid losing my life but also in how I was able to get the gun and turn it on my tormentor. But as for killing her, I have no regrets there because not only did she force me to kill my husband, but she broke her promise to me that I was to be taken back to my children if I did as she wished.

Nancy showed her true colours in lying, and that is why I am glad she is dead, though I also know she was merely acting out of a desperate, probably primal need for revenge. But after I had shot her and turned the gun on the man who was working for her, I forced him to tell me where Maddy and Alex were.

He gave me that information in exchange for his life and once he had, I told him to give me his phone. He was reluctant to do so until I reminded him that I would happily pull the trigger again if he forced me to, and once I had his phone, I made a 911 call. It was a call in which I told the operator at the other end of the line exactly what had happened and why it had before telling them I needed urgent assistance to get to a certain address to see if my children were okay. Unsurprisingly, given what I had told the operator, it didn't take long for several police cars to make it to my location by the river, a location I had given them based on describing exactly what I could see from where I was standing.

When the police arrived, I made sure to drop the gun because the last thing I needed was some trigger-happy cop getting confused and shooting me after mistaking me for a threat. But I did accept that I was going to most likely end up in handcuffs when they arrived and saw a dead body at the scene, and that was exactly what happened. But I didn't mind that because once I'd told them exactly what had happened, I said that I could prove my story was true in several ways. One, they could go looking for the warehouse in which not only the body of my dead husband lay, but where they would also find two members of the NYPD attempting to cover it up. And two, they could take me as quickly as they could to Nancy's address to find my children locked up in her basement.

That's what they did, and while there was a brief moment of panic when I feared I had been lied to again and Maddy and Alex weren't going to be there, I was thankfully shown that my children were safe and well when the basement door was kicked down and my two children were revealed on the other side of it. All I had to do then was go with the police to be interviewed formally and give a more detailed version of events of the day. But just before I could do that, I had been forced to tell Maddy and Alex that their father was gone.

It broke my heart at the time, almost as much as it breaks my heart now, to see the look on their faces when they learnt they would never see their dad again. But all I told them in that basement was that he had been killed as a result of Nancy's plot against us all, conveniently leaving out the part about me having to kill him and also his involvement in Nancy's son's death. But I knew I would have to be completely transparent when it came to talking to the police, though, even then, I had to make sure the officers and detectives I would be talking to could be trusted a whole lot more than the last ones I had been involved with.

Thankfully, not everybody in the NYPD was under the spell of Nancy Williamson, and as I sat in an interview room across the table from a couple of interrogators, I started from the beginning and told them everything.

Well, almost everything.

There was one small part that I left out of the story. I left out the part in which I knew about what Jack did to Conrad back in 2008. Aware that admitting I had kept such a secret about a hit and run case would likely result in a prison sentence for me, I kept that quiet. Instead, I altered the story somewhat to give me a better chance of being allowed to leave so I could return to England with my children.

I told the police that after our children were kidnapped, I received a call from Nancy Williamson in which she told me what my husband had done to her son fifteen years ago. I explained that I was shocked and almost didn't believe her but had no choice when she told me she wanted revenge and the only way she could get that was if Jack died. From there, I was taken from my hotel to a warehouse where Jack was brought to me, and I was told to kill him. After wrestling with my conscience, I pulled the trigger to save my children, a grim decision that, while making me a murderer, also only occurred because I was put in an impossible situation for any parent. Because I'd killed under such extreme duress, I knew it was unlikely that I would be punished too much by the law for that. I also knew it would help my case if the police had been able to get to the warehouse and find that corrupt detective and cop trying to move the body, and that was exactly what happened. Thanks to the information I had given them, they were able to arrest those two shady figures in their force, and any police organisation worth its salt is always going to be grateful to anybody who can help remove a few rotten apples that hide amongst the good ones.

I also explained that Nancy had been about to shoot me before I got the better of her, and alongside Maddy and Alex being found locked up in a room at her house, it was obvious that she had been the conspirator of a very dangerous and deadly plot, and I had merely been doing whatever I could to save my life and the lives of my two children. That helped absolve me of everything I had done to get us through the ordeal, so I sit here now as a woman who has killed two people yet is free to carry on living without charge.

But just because I'm not in handcuffs for anything I've done, be it shooting Jack, Nancy or currently maintaining my secret of knowing about Conrad's death sooner than I pretended to, it doesn't mean that I've come out of this whole nightmare in New York unscathed. Not only have I lost my husband, but I must live with everything that has happened for as long as I have left, and that won't be easy. My conscience has been heavy for the last fifteen years, and it will continue to stay that way until I join Jack in whatever place waits for the dead after they have ceased breathing and stopped living. Until then, all I can do is try to do what is best for Maddy and Alex because they are going to need my full support as they attempt to pick up the pieces of their life when we get back to England.

I hope they can both go on to lead full and fruitful existences despite finding out their father killed a teenager with his car and covered it up for many years, as well as knowing their mother shot their father after being forced into doing so. That's a whole lot of stuff that could lead to decades of therapy and counselling sessions for them, but if there's any real justice in this world, they will find a way to move on without it hampering their lives too much. They deserve that because neither of them has done anything wrong, be it recently or fifteen years ago when this whole awful situation first began spiralling out of control.

I make a little small talk with Maddy and Alex throughout the flight, asking them how their film or magazine is, as well as commenting on the food we get served to stave off our appetites during the journey. But it's still very early days, and it's clearly going to take a lot more time before the three of us are conversing in the same manner in which we have become accustomed to. Before then, there is the small matter of Jack's funeral to arrange and attend. His body is going to be repatriated once the coroner has done his work and the police are satisfied with my version of events. That will be a tough occasion to get through, as well as being an occasion that is very likely to draw the attention of several journalists, both British and American, who will be keen for more things to write about when it comes to me, my family and the wealthy Williamsons, who have kept newsreaders on both sides of the Atlantic busy with all their reports on the juicy story.

I'm sure there will be plenty of members of the media waiting for us when we land at the airport, and after almost eight long hours in which I've spent even more wrestling with everything that has happened, I look out of the plane window and see the green fields of England.

We're almost home.

But despite being hours away from New York now, I will always feel like I left a piece of myself back in that city, and it is a piece I will be reminded of every time I look at my wedding ring on my hand or the family photos in the album at home, or simply the empty space in the bed beside me at night. Jack's body might end up back here one day, but his soul left him in NYC and that'll always be the place I remember him being, too.

But other than worrying about the media and adapting to life as a widow and mother to two grieving young adults,

I otherwise feel glad to be home. As the landing gear deploys and the green fields around the airport get closer, I allow myself to wonder about when I might fly out of England again and, indeed, where I might be going when I do. I also wonder if I will ever take Maddy and Alex away on holiday again. If I do, it will definitely be somewhere much closer.

Somewhere nowhere near America and particularly, New York.

Somewhere sunny.

Somewhere like Spain.

> That would be nice.
> Surely nothing could go wrong there.
> *Right?*

EPILOGUE

The sheer beauty of the marina was just one of the many reasons why so many people were happy to come here and moor their boats before taking a stroll into town. With tall palm trees lining the water's edge and whitewashed buildings sitting on a hill beneath a clear blue sky, there weren't too many who came here and felt the place needed a facelift.

It was a perfect slice of paradise in the south of Spain, a real gem of a find on a continent full of other pretty places, and as the man stepped off his boat, he was looking forward to calling this seaside resort home for the next few days. Or maybe it would be weeks because the man was open to changing his plans and going in whatever way his mood took him, and if he was to find that he enjoyed it here once he had explored a few of the bars and eaten in a couple of the restaurants, then maybe he would prolong his stay. It was no problem if he chose to do so because he was not on anybody else's schedule but his own, and his schedule was very flexible.

Of course it was.

After all, he was supposed to be a dead man, and dead men don't have any appointments to keep.

As he walked away from his boat and past several of the other vessels that were already moored here by other wealthy sailors like him, he smiled at some of the names that were emblazoned on the boats. Some of them were personal, perhaps named after their owner or someone who the owner was close to. Or alternatively, they were nods to something nautical.

Rosie's Dream.
Sarah's Sails.
The Blue Voyager.
Queen of the Water.
Goddess of the Seas.

The man liked some names and disliked others just as easily, but he wasn't too concerned about what people might think of the name he had chosen for his particular boat because, like everyone else, he had chosen the name that he wanted. The name in question was of the more personal kind, referencing something, or rather someone, who the owner had been extremely close to.

The man's boat was called *Teenage Dreams,* and on the face of it, it could have simply been considered an ageing man's longing reflection on the optimism of youth and how a teenager is full of dreams and aspirations in a world that is just waiting for them to grow older into. But that was not why this man had named his boat in such a way. He had chosen the name because it was a reference to his son who had tragically lost his life as a teenager and, as such, all the dreams that had died along with him.

The searing sunlight was momentarily blocked out as the man passed beneath the wide canopy of a luscious palm tree, but he was soon back under the full glare of the fireball in the sky as he moved on, walking up a set of steps before heading for the street where so many other people already seemed to have gathered. His eyes flitted between people sitting at sun-kissed tables with tall glasses of beer and plates of seafood before them to those milling around in some of the small shops, perusing the items and taking a brief respite from the hot weather before carrying on along their way. The man was more intent on finding a bar to sit and have a drink in after he had sailed here from along the coast rather than doing any shopping of note but before he got to a bar, he had to pass some of those shops. When he did, he saw something that caused him to stop dead in his tracks. For the first time in a long time, the man's heart was beating fast and his stress levels began to rise as he stepped nearer to the shop to get a better look at the front cover of the newspaper he had just caught a glimpse of. When he did, he got confirmation that the two faces on the front of the newspaper were those belonging to a pair he knew very well.

A pair he had not expected to ever see again.

A pair he hated and a pair who had caused him to take up the nomadic life at sea he experienced now.

Picking up the newspaper, the man stared for a moment at the faces of Jack and Lorna Thompson before reading the headline beneath their photo.

WIFE RETURNS TO ENGLAND AFTER NEW YORK NIGHTMARE

Desperate to know the full story, the man turned the pages of the paper until he was able to find and read the corresponding article and when he did, he was stunned to discover what had happened. After reading the article through a second time to make sure that he hadn't missed or misinterpreted anything, he felt he now had the full picture, and it was this:

His ex-wife was dead after a spectacular revenge plot had failed.

The man who had killed his son was also dead.

And the wife of that man had just arrived home with her children, clearly after having made a huge mistake in going to New York with her family in the first place.

Bob Williamson could scarcely believe what he had just read, and not only was it shocking, but it brought back so many terrible thoughts and feelings - things he had tried to bury deep down inside him when he had made the decision to fake his own death at sea and start a new life in Europe under a new name, well away from reminders of his troubled past.

After having tried and failed to kill Jack and his family by starting a housefire in England, Bob felt he was out of control and was on a fast track to not only his own destruction, but the destruction of everyone else around him. Unable to live with what had happened to his son and also the knowledge that the man who killed him had got away with it, Bob had gone out on his boat to escape his old life and start again. He paid for a man in another boat to pick him up, and after leaving a suicide note on the deck of his vessel, he was gone, making it appear to the coastguards who would eventually find his abandoned boat that he had willingly gone overboard and sunk to the dark depths of the sea.

After making it to Europe shortly after, Bob used the money he had squirrelled away in secret accounts to fund what he had done ever since, which was mainly sailing between various harbours in the southern Mediterranean and maintaining a very low profile as just another man in his sixties who enjoyed the quiet life at sea. Nobody he had met in the years since knew he was really the wealthy businessman from New York who had taken his own life years ago, and nobody who had known him back then had any idea he was still alive and well and living halfway across the planet.

His intention had been to spend the rest of his days living out his quite peaceful existence in the prettier parts of Europe, a way of life that ensured he wasn't dwelling on the tragedies of the past and instead, was able to find some solace beneath the sunny skies. But then again, he had not expected to see his family name mentioned in the newspapers today, nor read about what his ex-wife had tried to do, or that the man who killed poor Conrad and drove away from the scene had finally got his comeuppance.

It seemed Nancy had succeeded where Bob had failed, at least as much in that she had rid the world of that criminal who had taken their son at thirteen. But she had lost her own life in the process, and while Bob had stopped loving that woman a long time ago, he still felt anger now because he knew she had died trying to get some measure of vengeance for the boy they had birthed together.

But that wasn't the only reason he felt the old feelings of anger returning to him as he stood there beside the newspaper stand while happy tourists pottered around him, chuckling loudly and looking forward to another warm afternoon. He felt anger because as he stared at the photo of Lorna Thompson making her way through Heathrow airport beside her own children, he believed something he had believed for a long time.

She had to have known what her husband did in 2008.

Despite what this newspaper was reporting in that she had told the police she had no idea Jack had been a killer, Bob simply didn't believe it. He felt it was impossible for Jack to have kept such a secret from his wife for so long, and he still believed Lorna had known about Conrad, which was why she had been spotted at the youngster's funeral and also why she had moved back to England so quickly with her family fifteen years ago.

Just leave it. Forget about it, Bob. You're beyond all this now.

Those were just a few of the things the man said internally to himself as he continued to glare at the photo of Lorna in the newspaper whilst also thinking about how Nancy had joined Conrad in the afterlife after tangling with that damn family from England.

That was when he knew he was at a crossroads. He could either carry on as he had been doing and continue living secretly in Europe, sailing around and drinking cold beer whilst trying to forget all about the pain he had endured back in New York. Or he could pick up where his ex-wife had left off and try to kill Lorna, who surely deserved to die just like her husband had for her part in Conrad's death going unsolved for so long.

Which would he do?

Keep seeking redemption.

Or return to seeking revenge?

Bob Williamson did not quite know yet, though he did have a strong feeling it would be a mistake to give up what was a peaceful life now to try and make Lorna pay. Then again, mistakes were a part of life. People didn't always do the right thing. Jack hadn't, and Bob believed his wife hadn't either.

So maybe it was Bob's turn to make a mistake. Maybe it was time for him to plot his next course and, this time, set sail for England. The weather wouldn't be as warm there, nor would the harbours be as pretty. But there might be one thing he could get there that he couldn't get anywhere else in the world.

Final closure for his son.

If he did that, Lorna's 'nightmare' would not be over.

Her husband's mistake had clearly been atoned for. But in Bob's eyes, her mistake had not.

Not yet, anyway.

Would it ever be?

That was for Bob to decide.

THE END

Download My Free Book

If you would like to receive a FREE copy of my psychological thriller 'Just One Second', then you can find the link to the book at my website www.danielhurstbooks.com

Thank you for reading *Her Husband's Mistake.*

If you have enjoyed this psychological thriller, then you'll be pleased to know that I have several more stories in this genre, and you can find a list of my titles on the next page. These include my most popular book *Til Death Do Us Part*, which has a twist that very few people have been able to predict, and *The Doctor's Wife*, which became the #1 selling book in the UK Kindle Store in February 2023.

ALSO BY DANIEL HURST

TIL DEATH DO US PART
THE PASSENGER
WE USED TO LIVE HERE
THE DOCTOR'S WIFE
THE DOCTOR'S WIDOW
MY DAUGHTER'S BOYFRIEND
THE INTRUDER
WHAT MY FAMILY SAW
THE HOLIDAY HOME
THE BRIDE TO BE
HER LAST HOUR
THE PERFECT ESCAPE
RUN AWAY WITH ME
THE RIVALS
WE TELL NO ONE
THE WOMAN AT THE DOOR
HE WAS A LIAR
THE BROKEN VOWS
THE WRONG WOMAN
NO TIME TO BE ALONE
THE TUTOR
THE NEIGHBOURS
THE BREAK
THE ROLE MODEL
THE BOYFRIEND
THE PROMOTION
THE NEW FRIENDS
THE ACCIDENT

(All books available now on Amazon and Kindle Unlimited – read on to learn a little more about selected titles…)

TIL DEATH DO US PART

What if your husband was your worst enemy?

Megan thinks that she has the perfect husband and the perfect life. Craig works all day so that she doesn't have to, leaving her free to relax in their beautiful and secluded country home. But when she starts to long for friends and purpose again, Megan applies for a job in London, much to her husband's disappointment. She thinks he is upset because she is unhappy. But she has no idea.

When Megan secretly attends an interview and meets a recruiter for a drink, Craig decides it is time to act. Locking her away in their home, Megan realises that her husband never had her best interests at heart. Worse, they didn't meet by accident. Craig has been planning it all from the start.

As Megan is kept shut away from the world with only somebody else's diary for company, she starts to uncover the lies, the secrets, and the fact that she isn't actually Craig's first wife after all...

THE PASSENGER

She takes the same train every day. But this is a journey she will never forget…

Amanda is a hardworking single mum, focused on her job and her daughter, Louise. But it's also time she did something for herself, and after saving for years, she is now close to quitting her dreary 9-5 and following her dream.

But then, on her usual commute home from London to Brighton, she meets a charming stranger – a man who seems to know everything about her. Then he delivers an ultimatum. She needs to give him the code to her safe where she keeps her savings before they reach Brighton – or she will never see Louise again.

Amanda is horrified, but while she knows the threat is real, she can't give him the code. That's because the safe contains something other than her money. It holds a secret. *A secret so terrible it will destroy both her's and her daughter's life if it ever gets out…*

THE WRONG WOMAN

What if you were the perfect person to get revenge?

Simone used to be the woman other women would use if they suspected their partner was cheating. She would investigate, find out the truth and if the men were guilty, exact revenge in one form or another. But after things went wrong with one particular couple, Simone was forced to go into hiding to evade the law.

Having assumed a new identity, Simone is now Mary, a mild-mannered woman who doesn't raise her voice or get angry, meaning nobody would ever suspect her of being capable of the things she used to do for a living. But when she finds out that her new boyfriend is having an affair, it awakens in her the person she used to be. Plotting revenge, Mary reverts back to the woman she once was before she went on the run and became domesticated. That means Simone is back, and it also means that her boyfriend and his mistress are in for the shock of their lives.

They messed with her. *But they picked the wrong woman.*

THE WOMAN AT THE DOOR

It was a perfect Saturday night. *Until she knocked on the door...*

Rebecca and Sam are happily married and enjoying a typical Saturday night until a knock at the door changes everything. There's a woman outside, and she has something to say. Something that will change the happy couple's relationship forever...

With their marriage thrown into turmoil, Rebecca no longer knows who to trust, while Sam is determined to find out who that woman was and why she came to their house. But the problem is that he doesn't know who she is and why she has targeted them.

Desperate to save his marriage, Sam is willing to do anything to find the truth, even if it means breaking the law. But as time goes by and things only seem to get worse, it looks like he could lose Rebecca forever.

THE NEIGHBOURS

It seemed like the perfect house on the perfect street. *Until they met the neighbours...*

Happily married couple, Katie and Sean, have plenty to look forward to as they move into their new home and plan for the future. But then they meet two of their new neighbours, and everything on their quiet street suddenly doesn't seem as desirable as it did before.

Having been warned about the other neighbours and their adulterous and criminal ways, Katie and Sean realise that they are going to have to be on their guard if they want to make their time here a happy one.

But some of the other neighbours seem so nice, and that's why they choose to ignore the warning and get friendly with the rest of the people on the street. *And that is why their marriage will never be the same again...*

THE TUTOR

What if you invited danger into your home?

Amy is a loving wife and mother to her husband, Nick, and her two children, Michael and Bella. It's that dedication to her family that causes her to seek help for her teenage son when it becomes apparent that he is going to fail his end of school exams.

Enlisting the help of a professional tutor, Amy is certain that she is doing the best thing for her son and, indeed, her family. But when she discovers that there is more to this tutor than meets the eye, it is already too late.

With the rest of her family enamoured by the tutor, Amy is the only one who can see that there is something not quite right about her. But as the tutor becomes more involved in Amy's family, it's not just the present that is threatened. Secrets from the past are exposed too, and by the time everything is out in the open, Amy isn't just worried about her son and his exams anymore. She is worried for the survival of her entire family.

HE WAS A LIAR

What if you never really knew the man you loved?

Sarah is in a loving relationship with Paul, a seemingly perfect man who she is hoping to marry and start a family with one day, until his sudden death sends her into a world of pain.

Trying to come to terms with her loss, Sarah finds comfort in going through some of Paul's old things, including his laptop and his emails. But after finding something troubling, Sarah begins to learn things about Paul that she never knew before, and it turns out he wasn't as perfect as she thought. But as she unravels more about his secretive past, she ends up not only learning things that break her heart, but things that the police will be interested to know too.

Sarah can't believe what she has discovered. But it's only when she keeps digging that she realises it's not just her late boyfriend's secrets that are contained on the laptop. Other people's secrets are too, and they aren't dead, which means they will do anything to protect them.

RUN AWAY WITH ME

What if your partner was wanted by the police?

Laura is feeling content with her life. She is married, she has a good home, and she is due to give birth to her first child any day now. But her perfect world is shattered when her husband comes home flustered and afraid. He's made a terrible mistake. He's done a bad thing. *And now the police are going to be looking for him.*

There's only one way out of this. He wants to run. *But he won't go without his wife…*

Laura knows it is wrong. She knows they should stay and face the music. But she doesn't want to lose her man. She can't raise this baby alone. *So she agrees to go with him.* But life on the run is stressful and unpredictable, and as time goes by, Laura worries she has made a terrible mistake. They should never have ran. But it's too late for that now. Her life is ruined. The only question is: *how will it end?*

THE ROLE MODEL

She raised her. Now she must help her…

Heather is a single mum who has always done what's best for her daughter, Chloe. From childhood up to the age of seventeen, Chloe has been no trouble. That is until one night when she calls her mother with some shocking news. There's been an accident. *And now there's a dead body…*

As always, Heather puts her daughter's safety before all else, but this might be one time when she goes too far. Instead of calling the emergency services, Heather hides the body, saving her daughter from police interviews and public outcry.

But as she well knows, everything she does has an impact on her child's behaviour, and as time goes on and the pair struggle to keep their sordid secret hidden, Heather begins to think that she hasn't been such a good mum after all. *In fact, she might have been the worst role model ever…*

THE BROKEN VOWS

He broke his word to her. Now she wants revenge...

Alison is happily married to Graham, or at least she is until she finds out that he has been cheating on her. Graham has broken the vows he made on his wedding day. How could he do it? It takes Alison a while to figure it out, but at least she has time on her side. *Only that is where she is wrong.*

A devastating diagnosis means the clock is ticking down on her life now, and if she wants revenge on her cheating partner, then she is going to have to act fast. Alison does just that, implementing a dangerous and deadly plan, and it's one that will have far reaching consequences for several people, including her clueless husband.

WE USED TO LIVE HERE

How much do you know about your house?

When the Burgess family move into their 'forever' home, it seems like they are set for many happy years together at their new address. Steph and Grant, along with their two children, Charlie and Amelia, settle into their new surroundings quickly. But then they receive a visit from a couple who claim to have lived in their house before and wish to have a look around for old time's sake. They seem pleasant and plausible, so Steph invites them in. And that's when things start to change…

It's not long after the peculiar visit when the homeowners start to find evidence of the past all around their new home as they redecorate. But it's the discovery of a hidden wall containing several troubling messages that really sends Steph into a spin, and after digging deeper into the history of the house a little more, she learns it is connected to a shocking crime from the past. *A crime that still remains unsolved…*

Every house has secrets. But some don't stay buried forever…

THE 20 MINUTES SERIES

<u>What readers are saying:</u>

"If you like people watching, then you will love these books!"

"The psychological insight was fascinating, the stories were absorbing and the characters were 3D. I absolutely loved it."

"The books in this series are an incredibly easy read, you become invested in the lives of the characters so easily, and I am eager to know more and more. Roll on the next book."

<u>THE 20 MINUTES SERIES </u>(in order)

20 MINUTES ON THE TUBE
20 MINUTES LATER
20 MINUTES IN THE PARK
20 MINUTES ON HOLIDAY
20 MINUTES BY THE THAMES
20 MINUTES AT HALLOWEEN
20 MINUTES AROUND THE BONFIRE
20 MINUTES BEFORE CHRISTMAS
20 MINUTES OF VALENTINE'S DAY
20 MINUTES TO CHANGE A LIFE
20 MINUTES IN LAS VEGAS
20 MINUTES IN THE DESERT

20 MINUTES ON THE ROAD
20 MINUTES BEFORE THE WEDDING
20 MINUTES IN COURT
20 MINUTES BEHIND BARS
20 MINUTES TO MIDNIGHT
20 MINUTES BEFORE TAKE OFF
20 MINUTES IN THE AIR
20 MINUTES UNTIL IT'S OVER

About The Author

Daniel Hurst lives in the Northwest of England with his wife, Harriet, and daughter, Penny, and if that doesn't make him lucky enough, he considers himself extremely fortunate to be able to write stories every day for his readers.

You can visit him at his online home
www.danielhurstbooks.com

You can connect with Daniel on Facebook at
www.facebook.com/danielhurstbooks or on Instagram at
www.instagram.com/danielhurstbooks

He is always happy to receive emails from readers at
daniel@danielhurstbooks.com and replies to every single one.

Thank you for reading.

Daniel

HER HUSBAND'S MISTAKE by Daniel Hurst published by Daniel Hurst Books Limited, The Coach House, 31 View Road, Rainhill, Merseyside, L35 0LF

Front Cover Design by 100Covers

Made in the USA
Monee, IL
06 December 2023

48335485R00148